"Hut one, hut two, hut three."

Before Gadget had another second to worry, he felt the laces slam into his hands. Automatically he dropped back to avoid the rush and set up for the fifteen-yard pass to Paul, the left end. He frantically looked left, but couldn't pick him out. He jerked his head to the right, and all he saw was a mass of maroon shirts rushing him, arms in the air. A moment after that he felt the hard ground slamming against his side. His head cracked against his helmet, and the point of the ball dug into his ribs.

"Give me the ball," Ron grunted in his face. He tried to strip it away, but Gadget managed to wrap his hands tighter and roll on top of it.

"Never." He may have been sacked, but he wasn't going to fumble . . . no matter what!

QUARTERBACK SNEAK

S. S. Gorman

A MINSTREL® BOOK

PUBLISHED BY POCKET BOOKS

New York   London   Toronto   Sydney   Tokyo

A MINSTREL PAPERBACK *ORIGINAL*

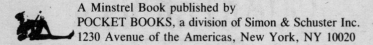
A Minstrel Book published by
POCKET BOOKS, a division of Simon & Schuster Inc.
1230 Avenue of the Americas, New York, NY 10020

ISBN: 0-671-70383-8

First Minstrel Books printing August 1991

10 9 8 7 6 5 4 3 2 1

A MINSTREL BOOK and colophon are registered trademarks of
Simon & Schuster Inc.

Cover art by Robert Tanenbaum

Printed in the U.S.A.

For my brother Tom
and his wife, Nancy

QUARTERBACK
SNEAK

Chapter 1

SEVENTH GRADERS

"Hey, ugly, what are you doing here?" Tall, lanky Stretch Evans stood up and shouted across Mike's Diner to his friend Chris Morton, who was standing just inside the door.

"Ugly, huh? Who you calling ugly? Takes one to know one." Chris met Stretch at their favorite booth in the back of the room.

"When did you get back from vacation?" Stretch held up his hand, and Chris high-fived it.

"Late last night. California was majorly excellent. Disneyland was the best, and I even tried some surfing. It's a lot harder than it looks."

"Lots of wipeouts, huh?"

Chris rolled his blue eyes. "You got it. I got a good tan, though, don't you think?"

Stretch held his dark black arm next to Chris's. "You got a long way to go to catch up with me." The boys laughed and sat down.

1

"So how was your summer vacation?"

"It's only August first. Vacation's not over yet."

Chris groaned. "I know. But didn't you just go camping with your family?"

"Yeah, and it was great. We went hiking and fishing. We even saw a mountain lion."

"Excellent."

"I thought it was really cool, but my sisters screamed their brains off."

Chris ran his hand through his wavy blond hair and looked around the room. "The old hangout looks the same."

"Yeah, Mike said he was going to fix it up this summer. You know, paint the front and straighten the sign. Alex was going to help her dad, but I guess they never got around to it."

"I'm glad. I like it better this way. The peeling paint and old chairs give it class." Chris turned his head toward the door of Mike Tye's diner. "Have you seen Gadget or the Klipp brothers yet?"

"Jack and J.R. got back from their vacation with their dad last week, and Gadget was supposed to come home from computer camp yesterday."

"So the whole gang's going to be here today. Great."

"Yep." Stretch's soft brown eyes gleamed with mischief. "Our first official meeting as seventh graders."

"Seventh graders—too cool! I can hardly believe it."

Stretch snap-popped his fingers. "Me, neither. I thought I'd never get out of Bressler Elementary."

2

"It feels weird to say we go to Dugan Junior High."

"Totally weird."

"Maybe it feels totally weird to you wimps, but I've been ready for years." Tough guy Jack Klipp had sneaked up from behind and now slapped the tabletop, hard. "Slide over." Jack and his younger brother by fourteen months, J.R., slid into opposite sides of the booth. They practically looked like twins with their dark brown eyes and hair. Until people got to know them, the only noticeable differences were the spray of freckles across J.R.'s nose and Jack's hair, which was wavy instead of straight.

"Finally we'll get away from Mrs. Dean's spelling lists, stupid rules, and—" Jack started.

"Me," J.R. said glumly. "Just say it, Jack, finally you'll get away from me. I'm stuck at Bressler while you guys live it up in junior high. This is going to be the worst year of my life."

"Sorry," Chris said sympathetically. "I always think that you're as old as we are. I forget you just finished fifth grade."

"It's all I can think about."

"Look, it's not like we'll be on another planet, or something," Stretch explained. "The schools are only four blocks away from each other."

"We'll still have the secret High-Five club meetings every week," Chris added.

"Plus we can see you here, after school. It's not really going to be that different."

"Sure, that's what you say now." J.R. slumped over and rested his chin in his hands. "I'll bet that

3

after the first week you won't even remember me."

Jack leaned across the table and squinted at his younger brother. "Who are you? What's your name?"

"Very funny."

"I thought I heard some familiar voices back here." A tall girl with green eyes and a long blond braid stepped up to the table. "I see the old gang is back together."

"Hi, Alex. How was your summer?" Stretch asked. "I thought you and your dad were going to spruce this place up."

"Too busy. I earned a lot of money helping my dad out here. I also went to tennis camp. I've got a pretty wicked backhand now, so if any of you guys want to play tennis, give me a call."

"Tennis? Who cares about tennis?" Jack said. "We're coming up on football season."

"Go, Denver Broncos, go!" J.R. cheered.

Alex sighed. "Do you think the Broncos will ever win a Super Bowl?"

"It's going to be this year, I feel it in my bones."

"You're crazy, J.R." Jack shook his head. "You'll be old and crotchety before those losers ever win a championship."

"Hey, show some respect for our home state team," Stretch demanded.

"Why should I? I rooted for those guys for three years, and they let me down every time. This year I'm sticking with the New York Giants."

"Spare me." Chris picked up one of the menus. "I'll always stand behind the Broncos, but since I was

4

in California this summer, I'm going to be watching the Rams, too."

"Bears, Chicago Bears all the way." Stretch rubbed the top of his short Afro flattop.

"No way," Alex sneered. "They've got a lot of rebuilding to do before they win any championships. I think the Raiders will be the team to beat this year."

"Gross. Those guys are just plain mean." J.R. leaned back in the booth.

Chris nudged Jack with his elbow. "Kind of makes you think about our own Raiders here in Conrad."

"Yeah, has anybody seen any of those creeps?"

Stretch looked over his shoulder. "How can you miss them? Ron Porter doesn't go anywhere without his gang of goons."

"Plus he's grown about a foot and has gotten even meaner," Jack added.

"Is that possible?" J.R. questioned.

"With Porter anything rotten is possible," Chris added.

"You guys give him more credit than he deserves," Alex said, shifting her weight to the other hip.

"Oh, yeah? Well, I guess you didn't hear about what they did to the Collins twins," Jack added.

"What?"

"Well, this is what I heard. The Raiders saw the twins tossing a football around in their yard. So Ron went over to Mark and told him to give him the ball. When Mark said no, Greg Forbes tripped him."

"Sounds like something Forbes would do," Chris groaned.

5

"That's not the end of it. Meanwhile, Randy Salazar and fat ol' Hank Thompson pinned Clark down on the grass."

J.R. winced. "Those guys are the worst."

"Ron pulled the guys' sweatshirts over their heads so their arms stuck behind their backs like they were in straitjackets."

"Bummer," Chris said.

"Not to mention embarrassing," Stretch added.

"Hey, I'm not finished yet."

"You mean there's more?" J.R. asked.

"You forget about scrawny Peter Farrell," Jack continued.

Stretch thumped his knuckles on the table. "He's a weasel. Sometimes I think I hate him the most."

Chris nodded his head. "He always lets everybody do his dirty work for him."

Jack waved his hand. "Well, this time he took the football and let the air out of it. Then Ron tossed the ball up on the Collinses' roof, and they took off."

"Poor Mark and Clark," J.R. said with a sigh.

"Just think, J.R., the Raiders won't be around Bressler to pick on you anymore."

"Big deal, neither will you."

"Okay, enough sob stories." Alex took the pencil from behind her ear. "You going to order anything?"

"What do you think," Chris said.

"The usuals, right?"

"What else?" Stretch shrugged.

"You guys are so boring. Stretch has a jumbo hot dog, fries, and a Coke. Chris has grilled cheese, fries, and a strawberry malt. Jack will want onion rings and a cheeseburger. J.R. will order chili. Who eats chili in the summer?''

"And don't forget the cheese and onions on top.''

"How could I forget, J.R.? You order it every time. And when Gadget gets here, he'll order—''

"Gadget will order a cup of minestrone soup, the tuna platter on rye, and an orange soda pop.''

The gang and Alex turned their heads to look at the tall, trim boy standing near their table.

"Who are you?'' Jack blurted out.

"It's me, Gadget.'' He tugged at his sandy-colored hair and blinked his hazel eyes.

Jack stood up from the booth. "The Gadget we know wears wire-rimmed glasses.''

"I'm trying out contact lenses.''

"The Gadget we know is kind of—well, pudgy,'' Stretch added.

"I lost some weight and grew.''

"I know—we'll test him. What's your real name?'' J.R. blurted to try and catch him off-guard.

"William Irving Shaw''—Gadget tried hard not to laugh—"but my dad gave me the nickname of Gadget because I like mechanical things like computers and video cameras.''

Chris leaned his elbows on the table. "It sounds like Gadget.''

"May I sit down now?''

"No way, Buck-o!'' Jack held him back. "We want answers.''

7

"All right, all right. You want statistics, you'll get statistics."

"Now, that sounds like Gadget," J.R. smiled.

"Over the past six weeks I have been at computer camp. During the course of that time I grew two and three-quarter inches and lost seven and a half pounds. The combination of the two elements, plus the contacts, has left me taller, thinner, and, therefore, greatly altered in appearance."

"It's Gadget, all right," Jack said as he slumped back against the booth.

Stretch agreed. "No one but Gadget talks like that."

"No one would want to," Chris teased.

Alex whirled around toward the kitchen. "Besides, he's the only person I know who orders a tuna platter."

"And likes it," Stretch and Chris said together.

"I've told you a million times, fish is brain food. It's good for your intelligence."

"Then how come fish are so dumb?" Stretch laughed.

Chris groaned. "Sit down, Gadget, and tell us more about camp."

"There's not much more to tell, except that it was totally enlightening. I've learned how to design a small system myself and feel comfortable with thirty-six kinds of software."

J.R. groaned. "That sounds awful. What's the use of being an only child if you end up going to school all year round? If I were an only child, I'd want a horse or something cool like that."

"We don't want to hear what you want," Jack fired

back and stuck out a hand, which he placed over his brother's mouth.

"Ah, some things never change," Chris said. "The Klipp brothers are going at each other again."

"Speaking of school," Gadget said. "Has anyone else been over to Dugan Junior High?"

"No way." Stretch cringed. "I don't walk into a school until the bell rings on the first day of classes."

"That's too bad. I was wondering if anyone else might be interested in the seventh-grade football team."

Jack sat up straight. "Football team? You mean they have a team in the seventh grade?"

"It appears so," Gadget continued. "A Coach Halligan has posted several bulletins announcing a seventh-grade squad. They're going to start summer ball practice the day after tomorrow. I was hoping to sign all of you up, but I thought I'd better check first."

Jack threw a napkin at his brother. "Unlike some people we know who signed us up for basketball without asking."

J.R. sat quietly.

"Hey, I'm up for football." Stretch nodded.

Chris shrugged. "I like soccer better, but if we all vote for football, I'll give it a try."

"A seventh-grade team sounds cool," Jack added.

"As I understand it," Gadget continued, "we'll be playing other seventh-grade teams in the area."

J.R. didn't say a word but slowly slid out of the booth and walked toward the door unnoticed by the others.

"I wonder who'll be the quarterback?" Chris asked.

Gadget took out the blue spiral notebook the High-Fives used for all their important information. "Stretch is the tallest. It's good to have a tall quarterback to look over the front line."

Chris smiled. "I don't know, Gadget, you're growing so fast, you'll be as tall as Stretch by the end of the week."

Stretch faked catching a ball. "Besides, I want to be a receiver."

"I want to be a halfback," Jack said. "Yeah, or a fullback."

Gadget jotted them all down in his notebook. "I figured J.R. might be an end or maybe center. What do you think, J.R.?"

Chris looked around. "Where'd J.R. go?"

"He was here a minute ago," Gadget said.

"You don't think he's upset because we gave him a bad time about the basketball team," Stretch said.

Jack shook his head. "Nah. That was no big deal."

"So, what's bugging him?" Chris wondered aloud.

"Of course." Gadget hit the side of his head with the palm of his hand. "It's a seventh-grade team."

Stretch shrugged. "So what?"

"J.R.'s a sixth grader. He won't be eligible to play."

"What are we going to do?" Chris asked quietly.

Jack made a fist. "I'm not giving up playing just 'cause he's not old enough."

"No one is asking you to." Gadget tried to calm him down. "We just have to think of a way to include him."

"Maybe we could tell Coach Halligan he was a transfer student," Stretch suggested.

"That's lying. Anyway, he'd find out because J.R. wouldn't be in any classes. It wouldn't work."

Gadget scratched his head. "I think I may have a solution."

"Great, spill it," Chris said eagerly.

"I'd better check with my sources first." Gadget jumped up from the table. "See if you can get Alex to put our orders on hold. If everything goes according to plan, I'll be bringing J.R. back here within the hour."

"According to plan? What plan?" Chris wondered.

Stretch sighed. "I don't see any way around this one."

"J.R. is just going to have to play soccer or play football with kids his own age," Jack said matter-of-factly.

Suddenly Chris sat bolt upright. "Where's Alex? I'm going to change my order to a tuna platter, too."

"What?" Jack screamed. "And break with tradition?"

"If Gadget can figure this one out, he is definitely the smartest kid in the world. I could use some of those smarts. If a tuna platter can give them to me, tuna's worth a shot."

"Yeah." Stretch smiled. "I'll change my order, too."

"Might as well make it tuna platters all around," Jack said and sighed out loud.

Chapter 2

ALL FOR ONE AND ONE FOR ALL

Gadget pushed open the heavy wooden door to go out of Mike's Diner. The warm, dry air of Conrad, Colorado, told him summer was still there. He didn't see J.R., but he was sure he couldn't have gone far. He started to push up his wire-rimmed glasses before he remembered he was wearing contacts. Old habits were hard to break, he thought.

"I'll check the park first," Gadget muttered to himself. He grasped the wrought-iron railing and swung down the front steps. He jogged over to the town park to find J.R. sitting cross-legged on one of the green benches. "Mind if I sit down?"

J.R. raised his head. "Aren't you too embarrassed to be seen with a measly sixth grader?"

"Not if he's my best friend."

"You're just saying that."

"You need data. I'll give you facts." Gadget cleared his throat and sat down. "Ever since we formed the High-Fives almost a year ago, we've been friends, right?"

"I guess so."

"What would I have done if you hadn't coached me through soccer? During basketball season, I was there for you. Nobody forced me to do that. That makes us friends. Look, Chris, Stretch, and your brother are all good in sports, and so are you. The only reason I'm in the club is *you* never gave up on me."

"And because you're smart."

"Smart enough to know that there is a way that you can be a part of the football team."

J.R. stared at him with hope. "How? I'm not brainy enough to skip a grade, and that's the only way I know of becoming a seventh grader."

"Will you trust me? Come to the school with me, and we'll talk to Coach Halligan."

J.R. jumped up. "I'd do anything to be a part of the team."

"All right, then, let's go." Gadget patted J.R. on the back, and the two boys jogged the few blocks to the two-story, traditional-looking junior high school. Gadget pulled on the front door. It didn't budge.

"It looks pretty closed up," J.R. said. "What do we do now?"

"The gym has a separate entrance. If Coach Halligan is here, he'll probably be in there." They walked around the building and passed several posters taped to the brick walls. They described the seventh-grade

13

football team, eighth-grade debating team, and all-school student council. A few mentioned orientation, and even one declared there would be a beginning-of-the-year dance.

"Junior high sounds like fun," J.R. said, reading a sign about the drama club.

"And scary."

"What have you got to be scared of? You're the smartest kid in school, and everybody knows it."

Gadget stopped walking. *"Was* the smartest kid in school—maybe. But that was Bressler Elementary. This is a whole new ball game here. You want to know a secret?"

"Sure." J.R. nodded. "And I won't tell anybody, either. I'm good at keeping secrets. I've got some I haven't told for three years."

Gadget smiled. "I trust you." He pressed his back against the redbrick wall. "I'm petrified to start school."

J.R.'s mouth dropped open. "You—afraid of school? I don't get it."

Gadget took a deep breath and let it out slowly. "I'm in junior high now. There's a lot more expected of me. Kids from the other elementaries will be coming here. They have guys who were the smartest kids in their schools, too. What if I'm fifth in the class, or tenth, or even twentieth? I'll never be able to face myself or my parents again. That's why it's important for me to do well on the football team and with the High-Fives."

"You'll always be tops with the High-Fives."

Gadget snapped back. "And so will you. Now, let's go find Coach Halligan." Gadget tugged at J.R., and they raced around to the triple set of double doors that led into the gymnasium.

"Bad news!" J.R. exclaimed as he pulled the first handle.

Gadget tried the middle doors with the same lack of success. "Maybe if we knock, someone will come out."

J.R. yanked on one of the third set of doors with all his strength. To his surprise it flung open, sending him flying backward and landing not too gracefully on the sidewalk. "We're in luck."

Gadget helped him up, and the two boys scrambled into the building. "Now let's go find Coach Halligan."

"This place is humongous." J.R. stared at the high ceilings and several rows of bleachers. "It's almost as big as the high-school gym."

"Hey, look." Gadget pointed to a lighted office at the far end of the arena. "I'll bet that's the coach's office."

They hurried over to the open door and spied a broad-shouldered man with wavy brown hair talking on the phone. "He has a nice smile," Gadget whispered. "My mother says a person can't be all bad if he has a nice smile."

"Let's hope your mother's right this time."

Gadget turned J.R.'s shoulders so the two boys were facing each other. "Are you sure you want to be a part of the team? You probably won't be allowed to play, but you'll be with us every day working hard."

J.R.'s dark eyes were serious. "Anything. I'm willing to try anything."

Coach Halligan hung up the phone. "All right, then, this is our big chance." Gadget gently knocked on the door frame.

"Come in," the low voice rumbled.

Gadget pushed J.R. in front of him and stepped into the office with pictures of teams and players and diplomas lining the walls. There was a trophy case at one end filled with gleaming golden symbols of Dugan Junior High's successes.

"How can I help you fellas?"

Gadget started to push his glasses up on his nose again. "Coach Halligan?"

"Yes," he answered, folding his hands on the desk.

"My name is Shaw, William Irving Shaw."

"Gadget, for short," J.R. spouted.

"That's right, and this is my good friend Jimmy Ray Klipp, J.R. for short. I'm here to sign up for the seventh-grade football team, and I'd like to talk to you about J.R. becoming a member of the team as well."

Coach Halligan leaned forward and smiled. "All it takes to be a member of the team is to have a good attitude, work hard, and have a desire to do your best."

"I've got all those things and more," J.R. said enthusiastically.

Gadget put his hand on J.R.'s shoulder. "There is a slight problem—well, not problem, exactly. I like to think of it as a hurdle that needs to be crossed. It's nothing serious, just unusual."

"Why don't you just tell me what the difficulty is, and I'll see if I can solve it."

Gadget started pacing. "I think it's important for you to know that J.R. is a top athlete, not just in ability, but in his willingness to learn. He has an excellent mind, and intelligence never hurts in athletics. He always goes the extra yard and would be and has been an asset to several team sports."

"But—" Coach Halligan interrupted.

"But the fact of the matter is—" Gadget started.

"I'm not in the seventh grade," J.R. finished. "I'll be going to Dugan next year. Now I'm a sixth grader at Bressler, but I'd really like to be a part of the team."

"I see. Well, that is a bit of a problem." The coach leaned back in his large swivel chair. "I'm afraid I can't allow you to play."

J.R. lowered his head. "Figures."

"Isn't there some capacity that he could help in?"

"We always need loyal fans."

Gadget paused a moment to think. "What about being the manager or statistician? He could carry your clipboard or be your gofer."

J.R. gave Gadget a weird look. "Gopher? What's a gopher?" he whispered. "I thought Dugan's mascot was the Mustang."

Gadget smiled broadly at the coach. "Ah, he's such a kidder. J.R. knows that a gofer is a special assistant who helps out the coach. He goes for this and goes for that—hence the nickname go-fer."

The room was silent for a moment until Coach Halligan pushed away from his desk and stood up. He picked up his clipboard and slid his finger down a list of names. "Hum, possibly, possibly," he mumbled. "I'll make you a proposition, J.R."

"Yes, sir," J.R. said, practically straightening to attention.

"The boy who was my assistant last year won't be back to help out during summer ball. I can't promise you anything once school starts, but if you'd like to help for the next three weeks, the Mustangs would be proud to have you."

"Yahoo!" J.R. jumped in the air.

"Excellent," Gadget added as the boys exchanged high-fives. He stepped closer to the coach and held out his hand. "You won't be disappointed. J.R. is a hard worker."

"And wait until you see Gadget play. It's amazing."

"Let's get you signed up, then." Coach Halligan handed Gadget a pen and the clipboard.

"I'm supposed to sign up my friends, too. We all want to play."

"Just make sure you're all here tomorrow at three P.M. We have our first meeting then. You, too, J.R."

J.R.'s smile was so big that his eyes became slits. "I'll be here."

"See you at three," Gadget said with emphasis as the twosome left the office and went into the gym.

J.R. jumped, karate kicked, and whirled around with excitement. "You did it! You *are* the smartest person in the world. I'm actually going to be a Mustang."

The double doors on the far side of the gym opened,

and a ray of light flooded in, silhouetting five shadowy figures.

"It must be the gang and Alex," J.R. said, taking off across the floor. "Let's tell them the good news."

The two only went a few feet before they realized it wasn't the High-Fives.

"Well, well, what do we have here?" Carrot-top Ron Porter stepped out of the shaft of bright light. His freckled skin was tan, which made his clear blue eyes burn like lasers. "It's the brain and the squaw."

"I'm not a squaw!" J.R. snapped. "I'm part Sioux— a Native American—"

"I doubt it." Randy Salazar, the strongest and most muscular member of the Raiders, circled J.R.

Greg Forbes blocked their way. "What are you doing here anyway, Klipp? Little kids belong back at Bressler." Greg's blue eyes flashed with mischief as he ran his hand through his jet black hair.

"Hey, look, Four Eyes lost his glasses." Tubby Hank Thompson stuck his face right up next to Gadget's nose.

"Yeah, and he looks different, too," Ron added.

Gadget stepped back. "I'm wearing contact lenses."

"Woo!" Ron faked being afraid and stepped away.

"What'd you do?" Scrawny Peter Farrell added. "Quit the computer and start jogging?"

"I grew a few inches." Gadget stood as tall as he could.

"So, is that supposed to impress me?" Ron leered.

"Come on, Gadget, we don't have to listen to these

jerks." J.R. walked past the group and made his way toward the exit.

"Watch who you're calling a jerk, pip-squeak." Ron's voice bounced against the empty walls and echoed back.

Gadget whispered as the reached the doors, "You're awfully brave today, J.R."

"If I'm going to have to face those guys every day at football practice, I'd better be able to face them now. Besides, after all the work you did, I don't want to let you down."

"Let me down?" Gadget squinted as they walked into the bright sunlight.

"Yeah, nobody wants to let his role model down." J.R. tilted his head up to Gadget and smiled.

Gadget cocked his head in surprise. Role model, he thought. He'd never thought of himself as a role model. Maybe seventh grade wasn't going to be so bad after all.

Chapter 3

THE LINEUP

"So it's official, Gadget?" Stretch asked from his spot on top of the park bench where J.R. had been sitting the day before. "We're on the Dugan Junior High School football team?"

"The Mustangs," Gadget stated proudly. "Yes, I believe so."

"And J.R.'s coming to practices, too?" Jack didn't sound very excited.

"At least for summer ball."

J.R. strutted like a peacock. "But I'm going to be the best gofer Coach Halligan ever had, so he'll have to ask me to stay for the whole season."

Jack groaned. "Over my dead body. When the three weeks are up, it's my personal independence day from you. I'll be at Dugan, and you'll go back to Bressler."

J.R. grabbed a clump of grass and yanked it out of the ground. "Well, you don't have to sound so happy about it."

"Why not? For the first time in my life I won't have my little brother tagging along."

"So are you guys psyched?" Chris asked as he bounded onto the scene. Everyone nodded. "We got worried when you didn't come back to Mike's yesterday."

"Let's go on over to the gym now," J.R. begged. "I want to let the coach know how ready I am."

"It's going to take more than being early to do that," Jack groaned.

Gadget decided to intervene. "It couldn't hurt. We could evaluate the other team members, get a feel for the field, and maybe practice a few plays."

The gang all nodded their agreement. Chris grabbed the ball and shouted, "Hey, guys! Go out for a long one." They scrambled in all directions, and Chris hurled a high spiral a few yards across the park.

"It's mine!" Stretch shot his long arms into the air, wrapped his fingers around the ball, and tucked it under his arm before tumbling to the ground. Jack tagged him on the back with both hands to secure the down. Before he could move, J.R. pounced on top of his brother, crunching him and flattening Stretch even more. Gadget piled on, and Chris made the final leap, completing the pyramid. "Personal foul," Stretch groaned.

"You guys weigh a ton," Jack said, trying not to laugh.

Chris pushed down harder. "Dog pile, dog pile."

Alex sauntered into the park and over to the mound just then. "You guys are pathetic."

"It's football." Stretch gasped for air from the bottom of the stack. "You gotta be tough."

Alex set her hands on her hips. "Right, real tough."

Chris toppled off the top and peeled Gadget and J.R. off, too. "It's a guy thing, Alex. Girls don't understand macho things like tackling."

"Spare me. I've played flag football for the past three years. Believe me, it's a lot harder to grab a strip of material flapping in the wind than to just mow someone down with brute force."

Gadget nodded. "Alex makes a good point, though. Most people forget that football is a sport that takes a lot of intelligence. You have to memorize playbooks, understand physics, and be able to move quickly with power and strength."

"Are you sure you're not planning to be the coach?" Chris said.

"Perhaps someday. It would be quite challenging."

Jack tried to rearrange his flattened hair. "Yeah, well, our challenge today is to get to practice on time and in one piece."

Stretch tossed a low lateral to Chris. "Maybe we should just walk over." The gang walked silently for a moment until they realized that Alex was still with them.

"What are you doing?" Jack snarled.

"I'm going to Dugan."

"For football practice?" Stretch asked.

"It's a free country."

J.R. squinted into the summer sun. "You going to be a cheerleader, Alex?"

Alex rolled her eyes. "Yeah, right. No, dumbo, I'm going to be on the team."

"A girl?" Stretch and Jack said together.

"Why not?"

Jack laughed. "It'll never happen, Alex—you'll get creamed."

"What makes you so sure about that?" Alex towered over Jack.

"Girls aren't cut out for football."

"We'll see who gets cut by opening day."

"I think it's an excellent idea," said Gadget. "What position are you considering?"

"It better not be an end," Jack snapped, "because that's where I'm going to be."

"Or halfback," Chris echoed.

"Or fullback," Stretch added.

"I could if I wanted to. I'm sure I could give you guys a run for your money."

"She's probably right," said Gadget. "You also have the qualifications for making an excellent candidate for quarterback."

"Q.B.? No way!" Jack mocked. "That's your position, Gadget."

Gadget blushed. "I'm not much at passing."

"Actually," Alex stated proudly, "I'm interested in becoming the field goal kicker."

"Oh, well, that's different," Jack said. "The field goal kicker isn't really a football player."

"Says who?" Alex's nose crinkled with anger.

"Says anybody who really plays the game."

Gadget shook his head. "I think if you'll stop and

24

think for a moment, Jack, you'll realize how valuable the kicker is."

"She's got you there, Jack." Chris tossed the ball into the air. "These days the field goal kickers make half the points."

"Sometimes it's the only offense against a good defense," Gadget added.

"Fine, she can try to be the kicker, as long as she doesn't get in my way."

"Afraid I might knock you down, Klipp?"

"In your dreams." Jack barely finished his comment when the group rounded the corner to the junior-high gym. There was a large group of guys clumped by the entrance, another by the wall, and yet another inside the gym doors.

"You don't think they're all here to play seventh-grade football, do you?" Gadget sounded nervous.

Everyone followed Chris into the gym. "This is worse than the soccer tryouts last year."

"Welcome to the big leagues," Alex said confidently.

"Do you think we'll all be on the team? I never thought they'd make cuts," Chris said.

"Don't worry, Morton, you'll be one of the first to go." Ron Porter and his gang, who were standing on the first row of bleachers just inside the door, startled Chris.

"Put a lid on it," Jack said, elbowing his way toward Ron.

"Just because Morton's dad and brother were big football heroes doesn't mean he'll be," Ron continued.

Gadget was quick to defend Chris. "And he doesn't have to be, either. He's an all-around athlete."

"Oh, and what about you? What are you going to do? Be the water boy?" Greg Forbes stuck his hands into his pockets, his elbows straight out.

"Water boy? No way!" J.R. cried. "He's going to be the quarterback, just wait and see."

"Quarterback?" Ron howled. "Of what, Miss Beasley's Ballet School? This is Shaw we're talking about here."

Gadget could feel his face turning bright red. He knew he wasn't a great athlete. He never had been, but he was taller now and thinner. He'd been studying football all summer and practicing, too, by throwing passes through an old tire swing at camp. He hadn't seriously thought about playing quarterback, but the High-Fives kept saying he was right for it. He'd like to shut up Ron Porter and his loudmouthed Raiders once and for all.

"That's right, Ron, quarterback. I'm going to play quarterback for the Dugan Mustangs. So get ready to eat my dirt."

Both gangs stood with their mouths open. This was definitely a new Gadget Shaw. It wasn't just the contact lenses, or the weight loss, or even the added inches. The biggest change was inside Gadget.

Chapter 4

THE GRIDIRON

"All right, men—and lady!" Coach Halligan shouted. "Let's quiet down and listen up." The players filed into the first few rows of bleachers at the Dugan gym and sat down.

Gadget could feel his stomach flip-flop with excitement and nerves. "He'll be a good coach, don't you think?"

Chris whispered back, "If we get to play, he's the best." They both smiled.

"Fifty-five of you have signed up to play ball, and I'll be able to use all of you in one capacity or another."

"Music to my ears," Gadget whispered.

"Thirty-five of you will be wearing the maroon and gold jerseys of the Dugan Mustangs. The other twenty might work with equipment or be a loyal fan and supporter of the squad. Each position is important."

"I think he just hit a sour note," Stretch mumbled back to Gadget.

"There are eleven offensive players and eleven defensive players on the field at a time. With special teams and substitutes I've decided to keep the team size to thirty-five. I'll make three cuts, one at the end of each week of our summer practice sessions."

Gadget glanced around the gym and wondered how many people figured he'd be in the first cut. Just thinking that made him more determined to make the grade.

"On the registration cards I asked you to list the position you're interested in playing. There can only be one quarterback on the field at a time, so some of you will be asked to try other positions."

Gadget felt queasy. He raised his eyes to see if anyone was staring at him because he had put down quarterback on his card. He was relieved that no one seemed to be even interested in him. He made a fist. I've got to start thinking more positively, he thought. If I don't consider myself quarterback material, neither will the coach. The High-Fives know football, and they think I should be playing quarterback. They could be right.

"Each practice will be designed to improve strength and endurance. Developing special skills and good sportsmanlike conduct are also top priorities."

Gadget liked the way the coach was talking. He figured if he were a coach, he'd say the same things. He really liked the man—the long purposeful strides he took when he walked, his arms and hands emphasizing the important points. He held the respect of all those listening to him. "You can't ask for more than that," Gadget muttered.

"What?" Chris asked.

"I can ask for a break," Stretch said, wiping his forehead with the back of his wrist.

"What a grueling schedule," Chris groaned.

Coach Halligan stopped talking and studied the roster a minute.

Gadget looked at his friends. He must have missed something while he was daydreaming. "We can handle it."

"I don't know, Gadge," Chris said. "This is a lot different from elementary school."

"An hour of calisthenics," Jack groaned.

"Followed by an hour of special drills," Stretch added.

Chris shook his head. "Memorizing playbooks."

"And having tests on them. I thought football was fun, not work," J.R. added.

"It's a school sport." Gadget tried to make it sound light.

"Then we have an hour scrimmage." Chris didn't sound very confident. "You don't think that sounds hard?"

Gadget stood tall. "I prefer to think of it as challenging."

Stretch stood up and raised his arms over his head, getting the kinks out. "You go right ahead and think what you want. Personally, I'm thinking of it as a death sentence."

"Then why don't you quit?" said J.R.

Stretch stared at J.R. as if he were crazy. "What? And give up the team? Never."

"I think it means we'll have to stick together and work harder than ever."

"Gadget's right." J.R. nodded. "Football's a tough sport, and if we want to be good at it, we'll have to be tough, too."

"Look who's talking. The kid who isn't even going to play," Jack muttered.

Gadget, his enthusiasm still high, tried to cut through what was going to be another Klipp row. "And we want to make a good impression starting junior high."

"You know the Raiders won't be giving up," Chris added.

"That's for sure. We can't get cut." Stretch sat down on a bleacher again. "They'd never let us live it down."

"So we won't get cut," Gadget stated.

"You sound confident."

"It's the new Gadget," J.R. said, patting Gadget on the back.

Jack laughed. "Tough as nails."

"As I said, it's a tough sport," said Gadget. "Look at the words they use: *tackle, kick, block—*"

Stretch interrupted. *"Bend, fold, mutilate."* The gang laughed.

Gadget started to push up his glasses once more, but caught himself before his finger touched his nose. "Where do you think they got the word *gridiron?*"

Alex had joined the group, and Coach Halligan was within earshot. "Looks like we're going to get our first lesson from Professor Shaw," Alex teased.

"The football field has a white line all around it, right? Other lines cross it every five yards, right?"

"Yep," Chris said halfheartedly.

Gadget continued. "These lines make the field look like a grill for cooking meat—a gridiron. That's why the field is sometimes called a gridiron."

A smile slowly crossed J.R.'s face. "Oh, I get it."

"Cool." Stretch nodded in agreement.

"What's your name, son?" Coach Halligan asked, sounding impressed.

"William Irving Shaw—but Gadget's my nickname."

The coach flipped through the index cards until he found Gadget's. "Quarterback, huh?"

"Yes, sir."

"Well, I like an intelligent quarterback. We'll have to give you a try."

Gadget couldn't control the wide grin that took over his face after Coach Halligan walked away. The rest of the gang gave him giant smiles of encouragement, too.

"Way to go, Gadget!" Chris slapped him five.

Coach Halligan blew his whistle. "All right, I'll see you back here tomorrow morning at nine, ready for action."

For once in his life Gadget knew he was ready right then.

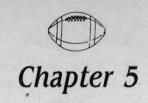

Chapter 5

THE WORKOUT

Prrt! Gadget thought Coach Halligan's whistle sounded loud as he started the last lap of the football field.

"This is awful," Chris groaned. "I don't know if I can make it."

"And it's only the first day of practice," Jack added between gasps.

Stretch seemed to be jogging easily beside the others. "It must be a trillion degrees out here. I thought Colorado was supposed to be a dry state."

"It is," Gadget said, wiping the sweat from his forehead. "The ozone problem is causing global warming that seems to be affecting us, too."

"How can you even say that word," Alex panted.

"What word?"

"*Warm*. It's downright hot. It feels like my dad's kitchen out here. You could steam clams on the field."

Chris gulped. "Please don't talk about food. After

an hour of calisthenics, I think I'm gonna lose all of mine. Why did we eat breakfast before practice?"

"Just get me to that Gatorade bottle before I die," Stretch joked. They all glanced at J.R., who was standing beside the supplies about a hundred yards ahead.

Jack glared at his brother. "He'd better give me a drink the second I cross the finish line."

"I'd fight you for it, but I don't have the strength," Stretch added.

"Hey," Gadget said, nodding toward the other end of the field. "If it makes you feel any better, get a load of the Raiders. They look worse than we do."

The gang checked over their shoulders at the Raiders behind them. Chris chuckled. "Hank Thompson looks like he's about to melt into the ground."

"I can relate to that," Gadget added. "I feel as if I've lost another seven pounds today."

Alex smiled. "Even Porter and Forbes are a little green."

Jack agreed. "Yeah, like they just got off the Rotor Ride at the Fourth of July carnival."

The gang crossed the finish line and tumbled to the ground. "Don't lie down," Coach Halligan ordered. "Walk around for a while. Your muscles will cramp up if you stop too soon."

Stretch offered Gadget a hand up. "Man, if seventh grade is this hard, I'm a goner."

Chris, who was still bent over getting to his feet, said, "I knew there was a reason I wanted to flunk that geography test last spring. I could still be going to Bressler with J.R."

33

The gang straggled over to the benches where J.R. was handing out towels.

"We can't drink this, bonehead," Jack said as he snatched the towel from his brother's hands.

"Coach's orders, towels first, water second. You guys looked great out there."

"You mean we looked *the* best," Stretch emphasized.

"All except for that Charlie Palmer. He got in three minutes before you guys, and he hardly looks tired. He didn't sweat much, either."

"Thank you, Pat Summerall, for that informative sports flash." Jack snapped his towel and just missed J.R.'s ankles.

"He seems to be an excellent athlete," Gadget said as he dunked his towel in a bucket of ice water. "I wonder what his approach is."

"He's probably not human," Chris added.

"That's it." Stretch snap-popped his fingers and went into action with a burst of energy. "He's from Mars and has got a whole bunch of bionic parts and stuff. He drinks special hormone potions that give him super strength. They've sent him down here to take back to his planet the secret of playing perfect seventh-grade football."

Alex laughed. "Stretch, you're too weird. I heard someone say he was a transfer student, but I think coming from Mars is a little too far."

"Whoa, talk about Mars and Martians," Jack said, pointing at Gadget. "What are you doing, man, trying to make us look like idiots?"

Gadget had taken his wet towel and draped it over his head. He was still walking around in a small circle, shaking out his arms and legs.

Stretch picked up the edge of Gadget's towel and peered under it. "He gets contact lenses and instantly becomes weird."

"I'm cooling off. It's a simple theory, even for you earthlings. In the winter we wear hats to keep heat from escaping off the top of our heads."

"You make it sound like we have holes in our heads or something," J.R. teased.

Jack punched his brother lightly on the arm. "Well, in your case, J.R., he's right. Big holes."

Gadget kept walking. "If wearing a warm hat holds the heat in, then wearing a cold towel should cool things off."

Before Stretch dunked his towel in the ice water bucket, he asked, "Is it working?"

"Perfectly. It's like being in my own personal igloo."

Stretch finished wringing out the water and plopped his towel on his head. "Ahh, air-conditioning."

"Get out of my way," Jack said, pushing J.R. aside. The rest of the gang pounced for the bucket, soaking each of their towels. In a matter of minutes the whole High-Five gang and Alex were walking in circles with white towels draped over their heads.

Chris plopped down on the ground. "I'm going to stay under here for the rest of the day." ·

Just then Gadget sensed they weren't alone anymore

and peered under the edge of his towel—right into the red, freckled face of Ron Porter.

"I knew you guys were incredibly stupid," Ron panted. "But now I *know* you're totally nuts, too."

Greg Forbes was out of breath. "Where's that puny towel boy?"

J.R. had forgotten about his job. He flipped the towel off of his head and tossed it on the corner of the bench beside the supplies. "Here, I'll get you some towels. Do you want to dunk them in the bucket?"

"No, but I think I'll dunk you in the bucket," Ron said threateningly. "Just to see if you can breathe under water."

"Lay off," Jack snapped, poking his head out of the towel.

"It's bad enough to have a sixth grader hanging out with us, but if he can't even do a simple job, he should be kicked off the squad." Randy Salazar sneered.

Peter Farrell was gasping for breath as he joined the crowd. "Yeah, and I'll tell the coach he's goofing off."

J.R.'s eyes were full of panic as he quickly handed towels out to the rest of the Raiders. "It won't happen again."

"You're darn right it won't," Ron stated, his face still as red as his hair.

"Don't let them get to you," Gadget said, draping his towel around his shoulders.

"Yeah, they're just jealous because we got through the workout faster than they did," Alex said.

"Looks like we've got some candidates for the first cut," said Stretch.

"In your dreams, Evans. In your dreams." Ron took a step closer to Stretch, his hand balling up into a fist.

"Remember, Stretch, no fighting." Gadget clutched Stretch's shoulder and held him in place. "Coach said anyone caught fighting would automatically be cut."

For a moment no one budged. "Hey, y'all, how's it going? Do you think it would be all right if I had a drink of water now?" The new kid, Charlie Palmer, sauntered into the scuffle. "What do you say, J.R.? It is J.R., right?"

Everyone forgot what was going on and stared at the dark, curly-haired stranger.

Stretch put his mouth near Chris's ear and whispered, "Maybe we weren't joking. Maybe he is from Mars."

"My name's Charlie Palmer, and my family just moved here from Texas." He held out his hand to Gadget and shook it vigorously.

"Glad to make your acquaintance, Charlie. I'm Gadget. This is Jack, Chris, Stretch, and Alex. I guess you know J.R."

"Yes, siree. We met when I finished that little run. He was the only one here to talk to." Charlie walked toward Ron and held out his hand. "Now, you look like you've played some football before. Why, back in Houston, Texas, my old team, the Bulldogs, would have gone nuts for a big fella like you."

Ron backed off. "What's the matter with you? How come you talk so weird?"

Charlie tilted his head back and laughed. "Funny, I was just gonna ask you the same thing."

Greg Forbes shook his head. "Bizarre."

Gadget walked over to Charlie and patted him on the back. "You'll have to be patient with them. They're the village idiots. We don't have too many new people moving to Conrad from Texas."

"Well, I hope I won't be the last."

Gadget smiled. "Well, Houston's loss is Conrad's gain. The Dugan Mustangs are proud to have you on the team."

"Yeah," J.R. echoed.

Charlie scuffed the toe of his sneaker into the grass. "Well, I have to make it past the cuts first."

Stretch flipped his arms in the air. "Are you kidding? If you don't make the cuts, Halligan will have to recruit a whole new squad."

"I wouldn't be so sure," Ron said, sizing him up. "You might be a real clod on the field."

"Takes one to know one." Jack chuckled.

"You keep out of this, Klipp," Ron flared back. "This is between me and the new guy."

Gadget bravely stepped up to Ron. "Maybe *Charlie* doesn't want to play your game. Maybe he'd rather concentrate on football instead."

"That's right neighborly of you, Gadget. That's exactly what I'd like to do."

Gadget led Charlie away from the group, who was

stunned into silence by his bravery. "So what position are you interested in?"

"This is only round one, High-Fives!" Ron shouted over his shoulder as he grabbed a bottle of water from J.R. He crooked a finger and his gang marched with him to the bleachers, where the team was gathering.

Prrt! Prrt! Prrt! Coach Halligan's whistle blasted three times sharply. "Gather 'round, Mustangs, and I'll introduce you to our next segment, the drill."

Jack cringed. "Why do I feel like he's talking about an electric drill?"

"Or a dentist's drill," Chris said, shivering.

Stretch agreed. "I just figure pain is going to be the main part."

"Listen up," Coach Halligan said, staring at Stretch. "Up here I've written the words for the essentials of football. *Agility, strength, quickness, speed,* and *intelligence.*" He took out a pointer and referred to his writing on the portable blackboard next to the bleachers.

Gadget flipped open his backpack and took out a pencil and his blue spiral High-Fives notebook.

Coach Halligan continued his lecture. "First you'll do a fifty-yard sprint to the tires. Do high steps through the tires to the jump ropes. You'll jump for one minute and then run twenty-five yards to the blocking sleds. They're designed to feel like oncoming tacklers, so get used to them. The next phase is the cones. Start on the right side and weave through the six cones, ending up at the football bin. At the bin you'll pick up a ball and toss it as far downfield as possible. The final stage is another fifty-yard dash to the finish line.''

"This sounds kind of fun," Gadget said, smiling.

"A real obstacle course, just like the pros on TV," J.R. added.

Stretch snap-popped his fingers. "We'll ace this part for sure."

"You'll be doing this every day, and although I'm not looking for perfection, I will be looking for improvement." Coach Halligan slapped his hands together. "Okay, I'll call off your names in alphabetical order. We have two identical courses set up, and you'll be starting at two-minute intervals."

J.R. was assigned to time the rope jumpers on the first course. He set his stopwatch and waited for the first team member to come rushing through. He noticed Stretch near the front of the line.

Stretch was a good runner. He whizzed the first fifty yards and only nicked a few of the tires. He kept the jump rope rhythm even and only stopped twice when he stepped on the rope.

"Keep going, Stretch!" J.R. cheered as he set the stopwatch for the next player.

Again Stretch raced through the next twenty-five yards, and then stopped as if he'd hit a wall when he reached the blocking sleds. "Uh," he groaned, barely moving the grid.

"Put your weight into it!" Coach Halligan shouted. "Use the strength in your legs."

"I think I left my legs back on the running track," Stretch moaned. Finally the sled moved, and Stretch

40

pushed it across the line. He weaved around the bright orange cones slowly but surely, picked up a football, hurled it a good distance downfield, and then tried to hustle to the finish line.

Meanwhile, Peter Farrell had come to a dead stop at the sleds on the second course. Greg Forbes had caught up to him now and both boys were pushing it.

Jack wasn't as fast a runner as Stretch, but he was quick at the ropes and amazingly smooth with the sleds. Chris's difficulties were the tires, the sled, and the football toss. "I knew I'd blow that football toss," he panted once back at the starting line. "That's why I went out for soccer last year, no forward passes."

Gadget handed him a water bottle. "I'm sure you did a lot better than I will. It's a good thing the coach is primarily looking for improvement."

"Hey, look, that new kid is about to start on course one," Jack interrupted.

Stretch pointed in the other direction. "Yeah, and Porter's going opposite him on course two."

Alex stood up from the grass. "This is going to be good."

"Let's get front row seats," Stretch suggested.

The gang scrambled back to the start of the course and waited for Assistant Coach Bozeman to give the starting signal. "Go get 'em, Charlie!" Gadget cheered as the race began.

The Raiders had gathered on the other side and were shouting for Ron. They were fairly evenly matched on

41

the run, but Ron seemed to have an easier time with the tires.

"Keep your knees up high," Gadget coached, and Charlie seemed to pick up his pace.

"That's the way to do it," J.R. said encouragingly as Charlie breezed through the jump rope.

Both boys powered through the blocking sleds. Charlie got the upper hand on the cones, and they both tossed a good distance. The High-Fives went wild when Charlie crossed the finish line seconds before Porter.

"That was remarkable." Gadget congratulated Charlie, who was hardly out of breath.

J.R. handed him a clean towel. "You sure showed Porter who was boss."

"I think you've done those sleds before," Jack said, glancing at Charlie sideways.

"It was nothing." Charlie blushed. "It's just a few muscles built up in the right places. Why, back home I'm considered kind of puny."

Gadget smiled. "Well, something tells me you'll do just fine up here."

The rest of the gang kept talking to Charlie, but Gadget realized he still had to go through the course. Since most of the guys had already gone, they were choosing up sides and cheering on their favorite player on each course. Gadget wished he was done. He didn't want to be the focus of attention, not his first time on the course, not on the first day. Maybe they wouldn't notice when it was his turn. "Quarterback," he mumbled. "What made me think I could ever be quarterback? I'll be lucky if I make it past the first cut." He looked around for a minute plotting his escape. Then he thought of all the things he'd told J.R., and Chris, and even Charlie. If he didn't go through with this, he'd never be able to face his friends again, let alone his own reflection. He took a deep breath.

"Next up on course one," Assistant Coach Bozeman called, "Gadget Shaw. On line two, Randy Salazar."

Gadget could feel his heart sink to his toes. He had to go up against the biggest and strongest Raider of all.

Chapter 6

LUCKY CHARM

Gadget slowly walked to the starting line of course number one. He tried to shake out his arms and legs to release the tension, but they were shaking too much on their own. He took a deep breath and glanced back over his shoulder. The High-Fives, Charlie, and Alex all had such confidence in him. He only wished he had it in himself.

"This is going to be a piece of cake," Randy said, laughing from the starting point of course number two.

"Theoretically, this isn't a race," Gadget tried to explain.

"Oh, really? Well, maybe you'd better tell that to the rest of the squad, because they've all come to watch me cream you."

Gadget didn't want to turn around again, but he felt as if some unseen force were pulling his head. What he saw encouraged him. More than half the kids had lined up behind course number one to cheer him on.

The High-Fives were definitely favored by the other kids.

"You can do it!" J.R. shouted before he went back to his post as timekeeper.

"Remember, brain is better than brawn," Chris added.

Jack flashed him the thumbs-up sign. "Leave him in the dust."

"He only thinks he's good," Alex added.

"Get the job done." Charlie's voice drawled above the rest.

Stretch flashed him one of his toothy grins. "The new *you* can *do*."

Gadget straightened up for a moment and looked at his arms and legs. He *was* a new Gadget. He'd been able to keep up with the High-Fives when they ran around the track. He'd never been able to do that before. Even during calisthenics he didn't get out of breath or tired. "I'm not an out-of-shape person anymore," he mumbled to himself. "I have to stop thinking of myself as pudgy. Like Charlie said, I can get the job done—if I really put my mind to it. Just because I wasn't that great in sports before, doesn't mean I can't be if I really work at it."

Randy started laughing. "Saying your prayers, Tub-o?"

"Maybe," Gadget said, crouching down into a three-point football stance. "Or maybe I'm saying them for you."

"Go!" Assistant Coach Bozeman shouted before Randy could say anything else.

Both boys bolted off the line. Gadget forced himself to concentrate on the tires ahead of him, but he could sense Randy off to his left. They seemed to be going neck and neck. When Gadget reached the first tire, he felt his balance shift too far in front of him. He was about to fall when he heard Charlie's voice.

"Keep your knees high. Get 'em up, up, up."

Gadget followed the very same instructions he'd given Charlie earlier, and suddenly he was bouncing through the rubber circles like a kangaroo.

"You're doing great," J.R. said when Gadget reached the jump ropes. "You're way ahead of him."

"Really?" He didn't bother to check, but picked up the handles and flipped the rope over his head to start to jump. Once again he could hear the High-Fives shouting encouragement, but it was Charlie's voice that rang over the crowd.

"Light little steps!" Charlie yelled. "Light little steps."

Gadget filtered out everything and focused on Charlie's instructions. He could see J.R.'s mouth moving, but all he heard was "light little steps" in his head.

"Move on," J.R. said as he slapped Gadget on the back to tell him his time was up.

Gadget started· his twenty-five-yard run before he realized Randy wasn't with him. He was still back at the ropes. Up ahead were the sleds. He'd never done them before, so he didn't know what to expect.

Thwack! Gadget hit the gold-colored cushion and bounced back, falling to the ground. "What was that?" he muttered, shaking his head. He could hear the Raiders laugh as he pulled himself up to try again. This time when he hit, it felt like an electric shock had shot up his arm, but the sled still hadn't budged. Again he heard Charlie's voice like that of a little guardian angel in his ear.

"Bend your knees and hit it low. Use your shoulders for leverage, and push with your legs."

At that moment Randy barreled into the sled with the power of a steam engine. The back end lifted off the ground and moved the sled as if it actually was on ice and snow. "Sucker," he shouted as he took the lead.

Gadget tried a third time, Charlie's way, and it worked. It was gliding to the right too much, but he finally reached the stopping point.

"Move it, move it, move it," Charlie's voice instructed.

"Arrgh!" Gadget shouted like an animal as he took off for the cones. Randy was halfway through when Gadget wove around the first one. But it didn't matter—he seemed to be catching up with him. Out of the corner of his eye he could tell that Randy was doing something wrong. It looked as if he was going the long way around the cones. Then the answer hit him: Randy had started on the left instead of on the right, as Coach Halligan had instructed. In no time the boys were neck and neck again as they approached the football toss.

Randy picked up a ball and with a smooth action hurled a spiral several yards down the field. Gadget's wasn't as steady. The ball waivered and tumbled awkwardly to the ground. Not a quarterback's pass, Gadget thought to himself as he began the last leg of the course.

The last fifty yards would determine the winner. Gadget had a head start, but Randy was puffing in his ear. Gadget strained every muscle in his legs to kick out a final effort. Once again it was Charlie's voice over the crowd that kept him going.

"Keep your upper body still, and push those legs off the ground."

Gadget could feel the difference immediately. He was putting less effort into running, but was moving faster. An inch here, a step there, and before he knew it, he had crossed the finish line a whole body length in front of the biggest and strongest kid in their class— Randy Salazar.

The High-Fives, Alex, and Charlie broke away from the rest of the kids to congratulate Gadget.

Alex beamed. "You were incredible out there."

"Fantastic," Chris added.

"I'll bet you put in one of the top times of the day." Jack couldn't hide the surprise in his voice.

Stretch agreed. "Yeah, every time you seemed to have trouble, something got you back on track."

Gadget smiled at Charlie. "I have Charlie to thank for that."

"Charlie? What do you mean, Charlie?" Jack quizzed.

Charlie shrugged his shoulders. "What did I do?"

Gadget tried to get his explanation out between gasps. "I don't know how to explain it actually."

"Try."

"Well, it's just like Stretch said, every time I started to fall down or mess up, I could hear Charlie coaching me, and it helped."

"Helped? Man, you just beat Randy Salazar, the biggest Raider of them all," Chris cheered.

"Heck, he's the biggest kid of all, except maybe Charlie here."

"Gimme five!" Chris cried.

"Gimme High-Five," Jack added.

"Me, too," Alex said, slapping Gadget's palm. "I'm up next against Hank Thompson."

"You won't need luck to win that race!" Stretch yelled after her. "All you'll need is room."

The gang all laughed except Gadget. He knew what it felt like to be chubby and awkward. In fact, until he finished his race that very day, he'd always felt that way. He thought about saying something to the gang, but he kept quiet and walked behind course two, to cheer Alex on with the others. "Thanks for all the coaching, Charlie. You were a lucky charm for me."

"It was nothing." Charlie blushed. "I'm no lucky charm. I just played lots of football, that's all. Why, back home, it's downright unpatriotic not to play football. I'm just glad y'all feel the same way."

Gadget stopped for a second to watch Alex go through the tires. "Well, to be perfectly honest, Charlie, I've never been much of an athlete. Just ask the rest of the guys."

Charlie quit watching the race and stared at Gadget. "Ah, come on now, you're pulling my leg."

"No, I'm quite serious. Until you showed up, I was

regarded as pretty hopeless. So, if you have any suggestions at any time, feel free to inform me.''

"Well, actually," Charlie said in a whisper, "I do have some secret weapons at home. You can come over any time you like, and I'll show ya.''

"When?" Gadget couldn't hide his eagerness.

"Well, how about after practice?"

"Perfect." Gadget extended his hand, and Charlie shook it.

Prrrt! Coach Halligan blew his whistle and waved his arms for the team to gather at the bleachers. "Not a bad practice today. Tomorrow will be our first scrimmage. Coach Bozeman and I will be making up two squads tonight. For the first hour we'll do some warmups and talk through a few plays. Then I think we'll be ready to mix it up a bit. So hit the showers, and we'll see you tomorrow.''

"Tomorrow," Gadget muttered to himself. "I've got a lot to learn before I scrimmage." He ran past Chris and Stretch to Charlie, who was walking with Jack and Alex. "We've got to work fast, Charlie. I've got to be in tip-top playing condition for that scrimmage.''

"Whoa, slow down. Don't worry, I've got a few tricks that'll make you look like a pro in no time.''

"Then let's get to it." Gadget pulled Charlie's arm, and the two of them ran to the locker room.

Gadget rushed through his shower and pulled on his jeans and Harvard sweatshirt. "I'll meet you out front, Charlie." He didn't say a word to the rest of the High-Fives but pushed through the locker room door and jogged into the gym.

"Hey, you looked really great today," J.R. said, struggling with two large duffel bags crammed with equipment. "I think Randy Salazar's still in shock."

"Thanks," Gadget said, thinking only about going to Charlie's house. He mindlessly gave J.R. a hand with one of the bags as far as Coach Halligan's office door. "See you later. I gotta go."

"But, wait, what do you mean, go? Aren't you going to Mike's with the rest of us?"

Gadget shouted over his shoulder as he kept running for the exit. "Not today. I've got to work out with my lucky charm."

Chapter 7

THE PLAYERS

The next day at football practice the team was stretching out. "I felt like someone had clobbered me when I tried to get out of bed this morning," Chris moaned.

"Yeah, my legs were a little stiff, too." Stretch slowly went down for another push-up.

Jack struggled on his next push-up. "You guys are a bunch of wimps."

"I suppose you're going to tell us you didn't feel a thing." Alex sat on the grass, ready for her sit-ups.

"Oh, why don't you go and be a cheerleader like the rest of the girls?" said Jack.

"Because I've got to stay here and show you how this game is really played."

"Spare me," Jack groaned before starting his sit-ups.

Gadget was glad that Chris and Stretch had admitted to some sore muscles. It had taken him five minutes to get out of bed that morning. Even his pinkie fingers hurt. A hot shower had helped, but he hoped no one would notice that he smelled like muscle liniment. The warm-up was helping, but he really didn't feel up to the scrimmage.

"We missed you at Mike's yesterday, Gadge," Chris said as he sat up. "I tell you, there's nothing like an ice-cold, foamy root beer after a long hot practice."

"Maybe today," Gadget said, trying not to groan. "I had a refreshing drink, too. Not as tasty as root beer, though."

Jack stood up with the others and started doing jumping jacks. "Yeah, where'd you run off to, anyway?"

"I went to Charlie's house. He invited me. He was giving me some pointers on how to throw the ball better. Did you know that if you hold the ball with your fingers spread down the laces, your thumb and index finger make a U?"

"I could've shown you that," Stretch said.

"Me, too," Chris added. "Having a dad and a brother who are football stars does come in handy sometimes. I'm not saying I can do it the way they do, but I know I could have shown you."

Gadget wasn't listening but went through the actions as he spoke. "Then, when you throw the ball, you let it roll off your fingertips directly at your target. That's what gives it that spiral effect. The toss is completed when you step forward with the opposite foot, and your arm comes across your body to follow through."

Jack's voice sounded a little hurt and angry. "I thought *we* were your buddies. If you needed some extra coaching, I could've told you what you wanted to know. You don't need Charlie."

Gadget tried to keep it light. "Well, Charlie was sort of my lucky charm yesterday, you know."

"Isn't that the name of some cereal?" Stretch joked. "Lucky Charms."

Jack glared at Gadget and stopped exercising. "A lucky charm is stupid. Even the idea of lucky charms is dumb."

"That's it for now," Coach Halligan called out. "Take your seats men—and Alex." He smiled at Alex. "I want to talk over positions and plays before I announce today's scrimmage line-up. First off, I thought you might be interested in knowing that we lost two players. They realized that football wasn't for them. There's nothing wrong with that. There are lots of other sports for kids to participate in."

Stretch elbowed Gadget in his sore ribs. "All right! That means he's already got the first two cuts from the team."

"Kind of," Gadget whispered back. "But if you recall, he has to cut twenty guys in three weeks. Three goes into twenty, six times, with two left over. One of those weeks he was going to have to cut eight guys anyway."

"Well, thank you, Professor, for bursting my bubble."

"Just giving you the facts."

Coach Halligan continued his lecture. "Football is a game of skill, timing, and a lot of work. Teamwork. The eleven men on offense work together as a unit to make a touchdown. The eleven men on defense try to stop the other team." He motioned to the blackboard and looked for his pointer.

"Here you go, Coach," J.R. said, proudly handing him the wooden stick.

"Thank you. We'll start with offense." He pointed to a chart drawn on the top of the blackboard.

RHB—RIGHT HALFBACK   RHB FB LHB
FB—FULLBACK
LHB-LEFT HALFBACK
QB—QUARTERBACK   QB
RE—RIGHT END (SE – WR-TE)
RT—RIGHT TACKLE   RE RT RG C LG LT LE
RG—RIGHT GUARD
C—CENTER
LG—LEFT GUARD
LT—LEFT TACKLE
LE—LEFT END (SE – WR-TE)

"The center has two very important jobs. First, he starts every play by snapping the ball to the quarterback, and then he blocks the player he's assigned to. He must be smart enough to keep the snap count in his head and avoid penalties, and also be strong enough to block."

J.R. turned around to talk to the gang sitting in the row behind him. "That might be a cool position to play."

"Nah, I'm holding out for one of the ends," Stretch whispered back.

55

"The guards on each side of the center"—Coach Halligan used his pointer again to indicate their positions—"have to be the quickest players on the line. They've got to be prepared to dash outside for a sweep and plow straight ahead for running plays. They're the leaders of the line."

Again J.R. turned around. "You're a great leader, Chris; maybe you should be a guard."

"I don't know, J.R." Chris shrugged. "You don't get to catch the ball. I kind of want to do some catching."

"The tackles lined up next to the guards are the biggest and strongest players on offense," Coach Halligan continued. They block like tanks, creating holes for the runners, and also do a lot of hitting themselves."

"Sounds like the perfect job for Randy Salazar," Stretch whispered to Gadget.

Gadget nodded. "He'd love every minute of it."

"Behind the center is the quarterback," the coach began.

Half the players started to react. Gadget couldn't believe that many wanted to be quarterback. He wished he'd put something else down on his registration card. Even with his lucky charm coaching him on the side, he didn't feel like he had a chance.

"Settle down," Coach Halligan bellowed. "I'm sure we all know about the quarterback, but I'll refresh your memories from a coaching point of view. I'm looking for a tall boy."

Gadget secretly held out one finger to keep track of

his qualifications. He was glad he'd sprung up those extra two inches this summer.

"Someone with intelligence who can remember the plays and call them correctly is also essential."

Gadget held up another finger. If I know only one thing, he thought to himself, I know I'm intelligent.

"Another element is agility. The quarterback has to be able to take the snap, pivot, hand off to the backs on running plays, or drop back quickly and throw on the pass plays. He must be clever enough to fake out the defense."

Gadget decided to hold out only half a finger for agility. It sounded like something he could do, but he would definitely need Charlie's help.

"The last two things I'm looking for are solid running and a good throwing arm."

Gadget's heart sank. He was good in the running department, but he didn't exactly have the golden arm the coach would be looking for. "Three and a half out of five," he mumbled to himself. "Better than half, but will that be good enough?"

J.R. overheard him. "You've got it in the bag."

"Next we have the running backs." Coach Halligan pointed to the two halfbacks and the fullback.

"This is me," Chris said, sitting taller.

"And me," Jack added.

"My halfbacks have to be quick on their feet, but not afraid to do a little blocking. They also must be able to catch the ball."

Chris and Jack nodded and gave each other five.

57

"My fullback will be bigger and able to run up the middle for the power play."

"Ron Porter," Stretch, Jack, and Chris said at the same time.

The coach glared at them before he continued with the ends. "Where the player is positioned on the line determines whether he is 'split away' or 'tight in' with the rest of the linesmen. He is called a split end—called wide receivers in the pros—or a tight end."

"This is you, Stretch," J.R. said excitedly.

Stretch nodded his approval. "You said it."

"A tight end is a strong, talented athlete who has to be able to run, catch, and block. Our split end must have good hands and be fast enough to catch those deep passes."

"I just gotta be the split end," Stretch whispered.

"I'll let Coach Bozeman talk to the defense, since he will be our defensive coach. For today I think it's important for you to know that the defense wins games. We'll be using the five linemen, two linebackers, and four backs in the secondary. Of course this can all change depending on the play, or the opposing team." Coach Halligan handed the pointer to Coach Bozeman.

Coach Bozeman was a tall man with straight black hair, brown eyes, and angular features. Gadget liked him because he wore wire-framed glasses as he did, or at least as he had. "The linemen will be our biggest and strongest players. We'll start with a right and left end, two tackles, and a nose guard smack dab in the center."

58

"Someone's finally found a job Hank Thompson can do." Stretch chuckled.

Jack nodded. "He's only big, though."

Coach Bozeman continued. "They stop the run, rush the passer, and if they don't sack the QB, they pressure him into a play he doesn't want to make. Next we have two outside linebackers, quick, strong, and fearless against the run and the pass. The defensive backs are assigned to stop the pass. Two cornerbacks to defend the sidelines and two safeties. The strong safety sticks with the offensive ends, and the free safety is ready to pick up any stragglers. It's complicated, but that's why I'm here and we have practice."

J.R. turned to Gadget. "It does sound complicated. I may need some help."

"I've got a great computer disk that explains it. I know it inside and out, so you can ask me anything."

Coach Halligan took the pointer from Coach Bozeman. "The last group of players that we have is the specialty teams."

"Now you're talking," Alex said loud enough for everyone to hear. "Enough of this big-guy talk, let's talk skill."

Coach Halligan laughed. "Alex is right. It takes a lot of skill to be a placekicker, holder, center, punter, or returner. They have to be ready at all times, even when they're on the bench. When they're called in, they have to perform in top shape instantly. I think we all know that a lot of championships have been won on a field goal."

"Or lost," Stretch added.

59

Coach Halligan nodded. "Well, here's the moment you've all been waiting for." He took the lower edge of the blackboard and flipped it over.

The two diagrams looked the same as the ones on the front, Gadget thought. Then he blinked again and realized that instead of the positions, names of players were in their places. Names of the kids who would be playing in that day's scrimmage. Suddenly all his aches and pains disappeared, and Gadget desperately wanted to see his name. He closed his eyes for a moment, and when he opened them, he stared right at the spot where the quarterback would be. In bold chalk print he read, "Gadget Shaw—QB." He tried to push his imaginary glasses up again to make sure he was reading it right. He had read it correctly—he was really going to be the quarterback!

"I knew it!" J.R. said as he sprung up from his seat to congratulate Gadget.

"Look at that." Stretch pointed to his name. It says split end, Stretch Evans."

"That's not half as cool as the halfbacks," Jack interrupted. "Chris is on the right and I'm on the left." The two boys high-fived each other.

Alex pointed to her name as placekicker. "I guess I'll just have to be twice as good as I thought. With you goons on offense, I'll have to win the game with my power leg."

"Dream on." Jack laughed. "The only time you'll be on the field is after my touchdowns."

Gadget still sat there, just staring at the blackboard. He couldn't believe it. He didn't even hear the High-

Fives joking and cheering around him. Suddenly a voice snapped him out of his trance.

"Well, I guess you got your wish," Charlie drawled. "You're going to be the Mustangs' quarterback."

"At least for today." Gadget sighed. "Charlie, I'm sure going to need your help."

"You got it. Besides, I'll be standing right behind you. You're looking at the new fullback, just like I wanted."

Gadget stood up. "Charlie, that's great. I was so busy thinking about myself that I forgot to ask you."

"Hey, you're the quarterback, you deserve the attention."

"Right now I need to give some attention to throwing that football. Could you give me a few pointers before we start?"

Jack stepped closer to the pair and tried to congratulate them. "Nice going, quarterback," he said, but Gadget didn't hear. He was pointing to the side of the bleachers, and the two boys headed away from the rest of the team. Jack glumly watched them leave.

Charlie grabbed his football. "I brought you some more of my power potion to drink before the scrimmage."

"Great, I need all the help I can get to pump on."

"Potion?" Jack whispered to himself. "What kind of power potion would Gadget need?" He walked to the edge of the bleachers and peered over at Gadget and the new kid tucked out of the way. Charlie took a bottle out of his backpack and handed it to Gadget. Then he handed him two small pills. Gadget stole a quick glance over his shoulder to see if anyone was around, then he popped the pills into his mouth and drank the liquid.

"Power potion, my eye," Jack groaned. "Palmer's got Gadget taking drugs." Jack peered over at the High-Fives, who were still whooping excitedly about their new positions. I've got to be sure before I talk to Gadget, he thought. This is going to take some investigating, and I'm going to need the other High-Fives.

Chapter 8

BIG-PLAY CHARLIE

Jack didn't have a chance to mention the power potion or the pills to the gang before it was time to break up into teams and start working. The only things working in Ron Porter's gang was their mouths, though.

"Well, you know the really tough guys like Mike Singletary and Mark Gastineau are always on defense." Randy was towering over Chris as he spoke.

Tall, skinny Greg Forbes was strutting around Jack, his long black hair flying. "Like the coach said, defense wins games."

"I think strong safety matches my personality perfectly. I'm *strong* and it's *safe* to assume I'll be intercepting any passes Shaw can toss past the line of scrimmage." Ron sneered.

"I'm still holding out for fullback when the coach makes up the real teams, but for today it'll be cool to cream this lame-o offense," Randy said.

"Randy, you talk big, but let's see how you do on

the field," Chris said before joining the rest of the offense with Coach Halligan. The two groups separated, each going to a coach for instructions.

Coach Halligan cleared his throat. "For today I want to put together a sample of the plays we'll be developing."

"A long pass to the split end," Stretch volunteered.

"A lateral to the right halfback," Jack added.

Chris didn't want to be left out. "And don't forget the importance of a short pass to your powerhouse left halfback." He smiled broadly at his suggestion.

"I think we'll have enough plays for everyone, but don't forget the importance of our running game."

Gadget was relieved. He wasn't sure of his arm, but he figured he'd be all right with the handoff. Besides, Charlie Palmer would be his fullback. "I'll do my best on all the plays."

"Glad to hear it." Coach Halligan turned the blackboard toward his team and away from the defense, who was working on its own strategy with Coach Bozeman. "The offense will be wearing gold T-shirts and the defense will be in maroon." For almost an hour Gadget and the others listened as Coach Halligan mapped out the details of the Mustang offense. Gadget wrote each one in his notebook. He had to pry his cramped fingers from his pencil when they finally stopped to get ready for the game.

Gadget wiped his hands on his jeans. He hoped the sweat wouldn't cause him to fumble the ball. He nervously shuffled his feet trying to keep the new plays in his head. "Red Bullet four means to take the snap, drop back, and pass to Jack ten yards away. Okay, Pied Piper one means to take the snap, pivot to the right, and hand off to Charlie for the big play. Then there's the long pass to Stretch, called Screaming Eagle—I hope I can do that," he continued to mumble.

"You'll be great," J.R. said with a smile.

"You're not just saying that, are you?" Gadget asked as he slipped on some shoulder pads and a helmet.

"Hey, I'm your best friend."

"Thanks." Gadget fidgeted with the laces in the front of the pads. "How do these things work?"

"I know." J.R. started to show him.

"Here, I'll show you." Charlie Palmer stepped between the boys, flipped on his own equipment, and quickly crisscrossed the laces on his pads. "Just takes a little practice, that's all. You'll get the hang of it."

J.R. focused on the ground at his feet. "I could've showed you how—after all, it is my job," he muttered.

Gadget didn't hear him, so he picked up his gold shirt and turned to Charlie for more advice. "Do you think the coach will want me to start off with a long fake to the ends or try a quarterback sneak?"

Charlie led Gadget away from J.R. "Could be a running play to test out the defensive strengths and weaknesses."

"Let's practice some handoffs, then," Gadget said.

"Do we look cool, or what?" Stretch asked J.R. after Charlie and Gadget had left. He pranced around in his gold shirt and equipment.

"*You* look like 'or what,' " Jack teased.

Chris adjusted his helmet and popped in his mouth-piece. "I fill hafn't gutt'n ust to all dis ubber in I outh."

"What?" the boys asked.

Chris spit out the guard and let it dangle from the helmet protector. "I said, I still haven't gotten used to all this rubber in my mouth. No wonder I like soccer better. Football has too much junk to put on."

"But check it out, we look like hulks in all this 'junk,' twice as big as we do without it." Stretch threw back his shoulders and strutted.

Jack shook his head. "Yeah, but so does the defense." He pointed to the Raiders and the rest of the defense who were working out, pushing the sleds and tackling. For a moment the gang just stood still watching the destruction.

"Where's Gadget?" Stretch asked. "Maybe we should go over some of these new plays."

"We could use this extra time," Chris added.

Jack agreed. "Yeah, who knows if he can even pass a ball."

J.R. pointed toward Gadget and Charlie practicing handoffs. "I think he's already got the idea."

"Come on, let's go over to them."

"I don't know about this new kid," Jack said carefully, wondering how to mention the pills. "There are a few things about him I don't like."

"Ah, you're just jealous 'cause he's so big," Chris teased.

"I am not. It's something else—something creepy or sneaky."

Stretch laughed. "You've got a bigger imagination than me." The gang started to jog toward Gadget, but Coach Halligan blew his whistle to start the scrimmage. They gathered around him for a few last-minute instructions. "Alex will kick off and try to get the best possible position with the help of the specialty team."

Gadget didn't know too many of the kids on the specialty team. Eric and Mike were on the soccer team last fall, and, of course, he knew scrawny Peter Farrell from the Raiders. Gadget hoped Peter wouldn't get his hands on the ball—he'd probably fumble on purpose, to help his buddies.

Coach Halligan continued. "Let's start with Dodge City six, mix it up with Tinhorn Alley, and then depending on our field position, go for Screaming Eagle or Pied Piper one."

Gadget nodded his head. At least I can still remember the plays at this point, he thought. Maybe I can be an intelligent quarterback.

"From then on Alex will be running in the plays. Okay—huddle up!" he shouted. The offense piled their hands on top of one another's. "All for one and one for all."

Gadget's mouth dropped open. He couldn't believe the Mustangs' cheer was the same as the High-Fives'. The teams lined up on the sidelines and started to cheer each other on.

"Boot it a good one, Alex!" Stretch shouted through his hands to encourage her.

"Yeah, and then run it back a mile," Chris added.

"I'll need all the help I can get," Gadget muttered to himself.

Coach Bozeman set up the kicking tee on the fifty-yard line, and the defense lined up on either side of Alex.

"No helping your friends!" Ron shouted ten yards behind her.

Alex sneered at him. "I'm here to do a job."

"Just make sure you do it," Greg added.

Hank shook his head. "Who ever heard of a girl kicker?"

Coach Bozeman blew the whistle, and Alex held up one arm to tell the teams she was about to start. She used a short stride beginning with her right foot, her kicking foot. One, two, three, four, one, two, kick, her rhythm changed slightly on the last two steps. Her head was down, and her eyes stayed riveted on the spot where the ball was, even after she kicked it. Her follow-through was swift and smooth. The scrimmage was on.

Ron and the rest of the gang tore downfield like rockets. The ball hung slightly in the air, making it harder for the offense. When it finally did drop, Eric was ready for it at the fifteen-yard line. Alex had definitely proved she could kick a ball.

Eric tucked the ball under his left arm and protected it with his right. The rest of the squad formed a wall around him and powered forward trying to head off blockers. It worked well, until Eric reached the twenty-two-yard line and Ron Porter. He had to butt Eric only once before he sent him flat on his back.

Gadget and the other High-Fives stood stunned. "I guess in the long run it'll be good to have Ron on the same team."

Chris stared straight ahead. "Yeah, but these scrimmages are going to be murder."

"I don't like it." Jack frowned. "There's something wrong with us being on the same team as Ron."

"It's hard not to think of him as the enemy."

"He still is, man." Stretch slapped Gadget on the back, slipped in his mouth guard, and ran onto the field.

Gadget numbly followed and tried to concentrate on the plays. "Dodge City, Tinhorn, and then Eagle or Piper," he repeated to himself as he set up behind the center. Out of the corner of his eye he could see Stretch, and he knew that Jack, Chris, and Charlie were right behind him to back him up. Or pick him up. He took a deep breath and hoped for the best. The front line snapped into their three-point stances. The knuckles of their right hands poised on the grass, their left elbows resting on their left thighs for balance. Their knees were bent and ready to spring into action. Gadget placed his hands under the center's butt, his right hand on top ready to receive the ball. He could hear his heart pounding in the echo of his helmet. He'd never been so scared. "Dodge City six!" he shouted to the right side of the line. It came out high and screechy, and Greg and Randy laughed.

"Dodge City six," he repeated to the left, much stronger this time.

The coach had devised a system to indicate when the center should snap the ball. If the number the quarterback called was even, the snap would be on half the number. If it was odd, it would be on the exact number. So for Dodge City six, the snap would come on three. Gadget prayed the center would remember. "Hut one, hut two, hut three." Before Gadget had another second to worry, he felt the laces slam into his hands. Automatically he dropped back to avoid the rush and set up for the fifteen-yard pass to Paul, the left end. He frantically looked left but couldn't pick him out. He jerked his head to the right, and all he saw was a mass of maroon shirts rushing him, arms in the air. A moment after that he felt the hard ground slamming against his side. His head cracked against his helmet, and the point of the ball dug into his ribs.

"Give me the ball," Ron grunted in his face. He tried to strip it away, but Gadget managed to wrap his hands tighter and roll on top of it.

"Never." He may have been sacked, but he wasn't going to fumble.

The whistle blew several times, and Gadget could feel the weight slowly lifted from him. He handed the ball to Coach Bozeman and carefully got up with a hand from Charlie.

"You okay?" Chris asked.

Gadget blinked his eyes twice and nodded.

"Sorry we didn't block better," Stretch added.

Jack studied Gadget's eyes. "You sure you're okay?"

Gadget took a deep breath. "Fine, I'm fine."

"I told you that power potion would pull you through." Charlie slapped Gadget on the back as the coach blew the whistle for the start of the next play. The gang huddled, and Gadget called the play. "Tinhorn Alley, on four." The team clapped their hands and rushed back to their positions on the eighteen-yard line. The sack had cost them four yards.

"Tinhorn Alley!" Gadget shouted the commands. "Hut one, hut two." The ball landed in his hands, and he pivoted to the left. He had only a second to lateral to Chris for the play. Chris was there, and when Gadget pitched him the ball, Paul and Tom on the front line had opened up an alley along the sidelines for Chris to run. Randy pushed him out-of-bounds on the twenty-five-yard line.

"All right!" Gadget shouted.

"A gain of seven," Chris said, giving Jack the high-five.

The offense huddled. "Now we need seven more yards for the first down." Jack was eager.

Alex tapped Gadget on the shoulder. "Coach says you can decide on the play, either Stretch's Screaming Eagle or Charlie's Pied Piper."

Gadget nodded as she ran off the field and studied Stretch. He knew the Screaming Eagle was the play Stretch would want to try. It called for Stretch to run fifteen yards down, cut center five yards, and catch the pass there. "Let's see" was all he said out loud.

"Come on, man, let's try the Eagle," Stretch urged.

Gadget glanced at Charlie, whose play was Pied Piper one. It was a simple running play up the middle, with the handoff on the right. Gadget smiled at his new friend. "Let's give the Piper a shot—they'll be expecting the pass."

"Darn," Stretch said as he stomped to the front line. The rest of the High-Fives were a little surprised and disappointed, too.

"Pied Piper one," Gadget called to both sides. "Hut one," he called, and the snap came to him quickly. He pivoted right, and Charlie was right there for the handoff. He hunched over the ball and charged like a locomotive through the opening space the front line had created. A moment later he left both Greg and Hank on their knees. He was passing the thirty-two-yard line when Ron and Randy finally pulled him down.

Charlie jumped up after the whistle and ran to Gadget. "Way to go, QB, you just completed your first first down."

Gadget could hardly believe it. "You mean *we,* don't you?"

The other High-Fives were congratulating him, too, until Alex ran in with the new series. "Seven, three, and then seven again."

"All right." Stretch snap-popped his fingers. "Now we'll get into enemy territory." Number seven translated into the Screaming Eagle.

The snap went fine, but unfortunately, Gadget's pass didn't. He made the fifteen-yard distance okay, but his aim was way off. It bounced off the ground almost on the exact opposite side of the field. "Sorry about that," Gadget apologized in the huddle.

"We'll get them this time." Chris tried to sound positive.

Gadget forced a smile. Number three was Yellow Jacket three, a fake handoff to Charlie on the left that Chris then picked up and ran right. "Let's do it." They clapped. "On three."

Everything started right. Gadget pivoted left, but then instead of a fake he actually handed it to Charlie, who made three yards before he was forced out-of-bounds.

"What happened?" Chris asked back in the huddle.

Gadget shrugged. "I'm not sure. I guess I forgot."

"Hey, y'all, at least we made three yards." Charlie grinned.

Gadget sighed. "Okay, it's time to try the Screaming Eagle again."

"I'll be there," Stretch said. "Remember, only five yards, but keep it in the center."

"I'll try my best." The snap went smoothly, and even though the rush was strong, Gadget seemed to be able to avoid them. He saw Stretch in the clear and then hurled the ball toward him. Or at least, what he thought was toward him. Instead it landed in the hands of Ron Porter. Ron pushed forward until Charlie pulled him down on the forty-yard line. Coach Bozeman blew the whistle, and the Raiders congratulated one another as if it were the Super Bowl.

Charlie ran up to Gadget. "Don't you fret over that. It happens all the time."

Jack looked at Stretch as they both ran off the field. "Yeah, but it doesn't happen on Charlie Palmer's plays."

The second squads of offense and defense took the field while the High-Fives and the Raiders headed for the benches.

"Tough break," Chris said to Jack as he chugged some cool water. "Where's Gadget? He must feel kind of rotten."

Jack flipped a towel over his shoulder. "I don't know. Last time I saw him, he was with that Texan."

Chris punched Jack lightly on the shoulder. "You mean Charlie?" Chris looked around. "Funny, I don't see either of them now."

"Really?" Jack jumped up and turned to peer into the bleachers where he'd seen them before with "the potion." He could see them crouched down low under the stands. Jack grabbed Chris's elbow and tugged him toward the bleachers. "Keep your head down and your eyes up. Something's going on with Gadget, and I want another witness." The two boys crept up the first dozen steps of the bleachers and peered down on the unsuspecting pair.

"This is just a booster to keep your energy up in this heat." Charlie handed Gadget two small white pills and another thermos lid of beige liquid.

"Thanks, Charlie, this is great. I'd be totally falling apart out there if it wasn't for you and your power potion."

"It's nothing. Glad to help." Charlie looked over

74

his shoulder, and Chris and Jack pulled back to keep out of sight.

"What do you think is going on?" Jack whispered.

"Looks like it's d-drugs," Chris stammered. "Gadget taking drugs? I can't believe it. What should we do?"

"Investigate. And if it turns out to be drugs, we have to stop it."

Chapter 9

EVIDENCE

"I don't believe you, Jack," J.R. whispered. "You're just saying this 'cause you're jealous of Charlie."

"What would I be jealous of?"

Stretch held out his index finger. "Well, first there's his size, and then there's his talent."

"Shut up!" Jack shouted. "This is serious." The boys all stood quietly outside the gym waiting to see if Charlie and Gadget would come out together. "Besides, I'm not just making this up. You can ask Chris if you don't believe me. He saw it, too, you know."

"It didn't look good," Chris agreed.

Stretch scratched his head. "Gadget did say he wasn't coming with us again to Mike's today."

Jack shook his head. "I don't like it. I don't like it at all."

"Well, I don't believe it." J.R. stood taller. "There's got to be a logical explanation."

"Well, I'd like to hear what it is, if there is," Jack said.

"Me, too," Chris added.

"He's probably just going home to rest his arm or read up on his playbook," J.R. said.

"Rest his arm? That's a joke," Stretch said and laughed. "He didn't complete one pass all day."

Jack felt pretty sure about what he'd seen. "It's got to be drugs, I tell ya."

"The only time he was successful was when it was one of Charlie's plays," Stretch continued.

Chris agreed. "Yeah, and whenever the coach let him choose a play, it was always one of Charlie's."

"Jealous, jealous, jealous!" J.R. yelled. "If Stretch had made two touchdowns instead of Charlie, you wouldn't be saying any of this."

"I've got the answer!" Stretch cried. "It's probably the payoff. Yeah, that's it. Because Charlie is giving him his special secret power potion, Gadget is forced to make all of his successful plays with him."

J.R. groaned. "That's ridiculous. Gadget wouldn't do that."

"Well, it sure looks that way to me," Jack snapped.

"I'm going to settle this once and for all." J.R. started back into the gym.

Jack grabbed his arm. "What are you going to do?"

"I'm going to ask Gadget if he's taking drugs."

"Whoa, no way, slow down." Chris stepped in front of J.R.

Stretch blocked the gym entrance. "He'll just deny it. Junkies always do."

77

"He's not a junkie."

Chris glanced over his shoulder. "Not yet, maybe. But we'd better make sure one way or another."

"What do you mean?" J.R. asked quietly.

Jack interrupted. "He means we'd better get evidence before we go accusing anybody."

"Jack's right," Stretch continued. "Besides, we don't even know what kind of drugs they are."

"*If* it's drugs," J.R. emphasized.

Chris nodded. "Okay, *if* it's drugs."

"So what's our next step?" Stretch asked.

J.R. lowered his head. "Gadget would know what to do. He'd probably have the answers already. And if he didn't, he'd know what disk or what book to look it up in."

"Well, I don't think it would be very smart to ask him now, considering the setup," Jack mumbled.

"Maybe not." Chris's eyes brightened. "But J.R. is definitely on the right track. "We'll go to the library and check out some books and use their computer."

Jack agreed. "Then we'll have our proof."

"Yeah, that Gadget's innocent," J.R. added.

"Get back," Stretch called. "Somebody's coming." Instantly the four boys dived behind the bushes that lined the sidewalk.

"I can't thank you enough for all your extra help." Gadget and Charlie stepped out into the fading sun. "You sure you don't mind my coming over?"

"Are you kidding? It's nice to have a friend in a new city. I wasn't looking forward to this move, but y'all have been so good to me."

"You should really get to know the rest of the gang, too. They're all great guys. Alex, too."

"Oh, I will, but for now I like this one on one."

"Ah, you're just worried we'll all get hooked on your power potion, and you won't be the biggest guy on the team anymore."

"Come on, now, there's plenty to go around." The two boys walked across the school yard in the opposite direction from Gadget's house.

Stretch's mouth dropped open. "Did you hear that?"

"Psst, psst." Jack motioned for the gang to gather behind the bushes. "Well, does that seal it, or what?"

"It could mean a million things," J.R. fired back.

Chris folded his arms across his chest. "Yeah, and one of those million could be drugs."

"Remember, Jack and Chris saw him take pills, too."

Jack slung his backpack over his shoulder. "I say we follow them and start getting more evidence."

"Then what?" J.R. said glumly.

"Then we go to the library and get some answers. If it points to drugs, we'll decide if we go to his folks," Chris suggested.

"And be a snitch?" Stretch asked.

"Better a snitch than lose a good friend."

Stretch leaned against the wall. "Maybe we should talk to him first."

"Maybe, but for now we've got to stay low and keep out of sight. Watch them close and get any information you can."

"Like what?"

"Like what shape are the pills? What color is the potion? Stuff like that." Jack led the group out of the bushes to the playground slide, where they all huddled close. They watched Charlie and Gadget go around the corner and down the block.

Chris motioned for J.R. to come with him, and the two darted behind an oak tree across the street. Charlie and Gadget were still in sight. In the meantime Jack and Stretch slithered behind another tree on the opposite corner.

"They didn't go down Elm," Chris said as he tugged J.R. to the side of a car parked in a driveway.

"They're not walking very fast. Where do you think they're going?"

"Probably Charlie's place, but nobody knows where he lives."

Stretch made a sound like a crow, and he and Jack made a run for a wooden picket fence three quarters of the way down the block. Gadget peered back over his shoulder, and the High-Fives pulled their heads in from their spying positions.

"That was close," Jack gasped. "Do you think he saw us?"

"No way!" Stretch cried. "We're still safe."

Jack stayed close to the fence but sneaked up to the top and peered over. "They're turning right onto Oak Street."

"Head 'em up, move 'em out." Stretch pointed to a pair of garbage cans on the corner of Oak. At the same time Chris and J.R. barreled for the same two cans.

"What are you doing here?" Jack snapped.

Chris tried to scrunch down lower. "The same thing you are."

"Well, get out of here."

"We were here first." The brothers shoved each other, and a lid from one of the cans crashed to the sidewalk.

"Dive," Stretch ordered. Instantly the boys flattened out, trying to become invisible in the grass. Chris kept his eyes up and watched Charlie and Gadget.

"What was that?" Gadget turned toward the loud sound.

"Probably a cat fight or some kids playing ball. Come on, it's just a few houses down." Charlie started a slow jog, and Gadget picked up his pace.

"They're running away," Chris said in a whisper.

Stretch pounded the grass. "They must've seen us."

"I don't think so. Gadget wouldn't run away if he saw us," J.R. stated.

"Well, the old Gadget wouldn't, but if he's trying to cover something up, the new Gadget might." Jack crouched behind the cans.

"Innocent until proven guilty," J.R. fired back. "That's what Gadget would say."

Chris sat up and looked around. "Doesn't Alex live on this street?"

Stretch pointed down the street. "Yeah, in that yellow house at the end of the block."

"Hey, look, they're going in over there." Jack pointed to a light blue house with black shutters.

"Let's move." Stretch crawled on his knees a few feet and then dashed for the Palmers' house as soon as Charlie and Gadget were safe inside. He ran to the side of the house, hidden from view by a row of trees and evergreen bushes. The others followed right behind him.

J.R. shook his head. "Okay, so now we know where he lives. How are we supposed to see inside? Unless one of you guys has Superman vision, we're going to be standing here staring at the walls."

"No, we won't, jerk face. Look at this." Jack pulled off a clear plastic cover that covered the basement window well. The well was a semicircle cut into the ground about three feet deep. It was a perfect spying place—if Gadget and Charlie went down to the basement. He jumped in. "Jackpot! Look at all the workout equipment down there—that's got to be where they'll be."

"Let me see," Stretch said, jumping in the gravel-lined space, too. "Totally cool. He's got everything in there. No wonder he's so big—he's pumping iron."

Chris lay on his stomach and peered in the top half of the window. "My dad doesn't even carry all that stuff in his sporting goods store."

"The guy's an animal," Stretch said a little enviously.

"Get back, they're coming downstairs," Chris called.

"Take it easy," Jack answered back. "Unless they look up toward the ceiling, they'll never see us."

J.R. sprawled out next to Chris. "See, he works out to get those muscles, he doesn't take drugs."

"Oh, yeah, then what's Charlie carrying?" Jack rubbed a clean circle in the dusty dirt to see better.

"It looks like milk to me," J.R. said.

Jack glared at his brother. "Since when is milk beige?"

Chris answered, "Since it's loaded with drugs."

The four boys leaned in as far as they could. Charlie handed Gadget two small, round white pills. Stretch nodded to Jack. "Now at least we have a description."

Charlie and Gadget sat at the end of the workbench and toasted each other with the thick liquid.

"So is the verdict in?" Stretch, Chris, and Jack nodded in agreement. "Guilty," they all said together.

J.R. stood up. "I'm going to the library. Anyone who still wants Gadget for a friend had better do the same."

Chris nodded. "J.R.'s right. Even if the evidence is overwhelming, we should back it up with hard fact." The other two got out of the window well and put the cover back. No one said a word as they walked to the library located near the park and in between Bressler and Dugan.

"Now what do we do?" Stretch asked after they stepped in the front door. "Somehow I don't think we can walk up to the librarian and ask her about drugs."

Jack motioned for the gang to follow him to a table by the card catalog and microfilm center. "We'll talk to the librarian only as a last resort. I've got an idea. Stretch, you go find as many books on sports and drugs as you can. Chris, you look up the same thing on microfilm. J.R., you see if there are any books that

83

describe what drugs look like. I'm going to check maga-
zines about sports training techniques. We'll meet
back here in twenty minutes.''

"Look at all this stuff," Stretch said, flipping
through a few books he'd found.

"I found a jillion articles on the stuff. It's creepy,"
Chris added. "They say the use of drugs in sports is
everywhere. Some coaches practically force players to
use drugs, thinking it will give them an edge. Kind of
a do-what-it-takes-to-win theory.''

"Do you think Coach Halligan believes in that?"
J.R. asked.

"Nah, he's a good coach. Listen up," Stretch said,
flipping open a copy of *The Miami Herald*, July 1986.
"It says some athletes use lots of different types of
drugs. "Steroids and amphetamines mostly. Steroids
are supposed to enhance muscle size.''

Jack groaned. "I suppose Charlie feels like he's giving Gadget a break.''

Stretch continued. "They say steroids may increase
blood flow and red blood count. They could enhance
reflex time and attention span. And finally increase a
tolerance to pain and make the athlete more aggressive.''

J.R. scratched his head. "Is that good?"

Chris sighed. "Maybe for a day before you get
addicted and die.''

Stretch cleared his throat. "There's more. This says
the dose is usually twenty milligrams daily in six- to
eight-week cycles.''

"Do you think that's what all those pills Gadget's taking add up to?"

"Who knows? It says you can take pills or injections."

Chris interrupted. *"The Washington Post* says some players take the 'juice.' Gadget was drinking that weird stuff, remember. And there are lots of drugs with long names that I can't pronounce."

"I bet Gadget could pronounce them," J.R. said quietly.

"Let's hope he isn't taking them," Jack fired back.

Chris picked up another article. *"The Tampa Tribune* says they're addictive—*very* addictive—so that six- to eight-week cycle is bogus. Steroid users become junkies, plain and simple."

J.R. was getting frustrated. "This doesn't sound good."

"This is crazy! These drugs are supposed to be used for cancer patients or people with anemia, not kids and athletes." Jack started to get mad.

"Oh, man, this is bad. Here's a list of all the side effects and bad stuff that can happen to you. You want to hear it?" Chris held up the paper.

"No," Jack grumbled. "But for Gadget's sake we'd better."

"Then we'll know what to watch for." Stretch tried to sound encouraging. I can't believe Gadget of all people would get hooked on this stuff. I thought he was too smart."

"He probably thinks he can control it," Stretch added.

"It's a drug. No one controls them—they control you," Jack said. "Every dope knows that."

"Okay, here's the bad news. They can cause liver damage, heart disease, hypertension, acne, baldness, and can stunt growth in kids."

"I'm short enough already," Jack said.

"You know what's even scarier," Chris continued. "In all these articles they mention people who have died because of steroid use."

"When they're old, though, right?" J.R. asked quietly.

"Wrong." Chris shook his head. "These were guys in college or professional athletes, and they were really young."

"As young as Gadget?" J.R. stuttered.

"Let's hope not," Jack said.

"Ah, here's something. The word *anabolic* means to build up. They call it the Frankenstein look. It says you get bony overgrowths on your skull, it thickens your skin, makes your hands and feet bigger, increases your chances of diabetes, and—oh, man, can shorten your life by twenty years."

"You mean Gadget could end up looking like Frankenstein?" J.R. said.

"Yep. You know what's weird about all this?" Jack asked. No one answered. "Gadget would be proud of us if he knew we were doing research."

"But who ever thought it would be about him!" Chris cried.

Stretch scanned another journal. "It says here football players are some of the worst abusers."

"Not John Elway," J.R. said quickly.

"He's too smart for that," Chris added.

"How do you test for this stuff? We may have to do that to be sure." Each boy flipped through his material, but Chris came up with the answer first. "Blood or urine samples."

"Which sometimes don't do any good because there are other drugs that mask the use of those drugs." Jack flung his arms up in the air.

"Do you think Charlie would have Gadget taking those, too?"

"I wouldn't put it past him," Jack said flatly.

J.R. shook his head. "It just doesn't sound like Charlie."

"We didn't think Gadget would take drugs, either," Chris said quietly.

Chapter 10

FIVE HUNDRED

"This was a great idea," Alex said as she leaned against the tree trunk and kicked her leg in the air. "Five hundred is the kicker's perfect drill."

"Well, we could use the practice catching, too." Stretch passed the football to Chris. "Other than puny short passes, we haven't gotten to catch any real passes all week."

"That's because when Gadget's quarterbacking, the only guy who gets the ball is Charlie."

Jack pulled his little brother away. "Are you sure he said he was coming?"

J.R. groaned. "I've told you this a billion times. I went to his house, and he acted perfectly normal. I told him we were going to play five hundred in the park by Mike's at three. Then we were going to have a High-Fives meeting and get something to eat. He said he'd be here."

"Alone?"

"Of course alone."

"Did he say alone?'

"Well, no, not exactly."

"Then you don't know if Charlie's planning to tag along?"

"Look, he didn't say anything about Charlie, so I figure he isn't coming. Besides, I said we were going to have a High-Fives meeting. He knows Charlie can't come to that."

Jack looked toward the park entrance. "Well, let's hope you're right. We'll never get a chance to talk to Gadget and find out the truth if the gorilla man comes, too."

J.R. started to walk toward the playing area. "He's not a gorilla man. He's a nice guy if y'all would give him a chance."

"Y'all?" Jack shouted. "He's taken you in, too." The brothers were about to get into it again when they were interrupted.

"This is an excellent idea." Gadget marched toward the gang, and close behind him was Charlie. "Maybe if I practice catching the ball, I'll be able to get a better feel for it."

The gang didn't hear a word he said because they were all staring at Charlie. "I thought you said he wasn't coming," Jack whispered sharply to J.R.

Chris shook his head. "How are we supposed to have a High-Fives meeting?"

Stretch moaned. "Forget the meeting. How are we supposed to talk to Gadget if his supplier is standing right next to him?"

Jack slapped his hand against a tree. "I knew we shouldn't have let J.R. do the talking."

"I asked Charlie to come along since he's on the team and all. He's got some great tips for playing ball," Gadget said, coming up to them.

"Like drugs," Stretch said under his breath.

"Hi, Charlie," J.R. said. The others glared at him.

"Hey, J.R.," he answered back with a wave.

Alex broke the tension. "Let's play some ball. Tomorrow's the first cut."

"Yeah, let's play," J.R. echoed.

"Okay, here are the rules." Alex tucked the football under her arm. "I'll face you guys and kick the ball. If you catch it before it lands, you get one hundred points. If it bounces once you get fifty; twice, twenty-five; and then it's a dead ball."

"What if you drop the ball?" Gadget asked.

"We tell Coach Halligan, and you get cut from the team." Jack sounded deadly serious.

"You deduct points," Alex continued. "Drop it from the air, minus a hundred; one bounce, fifty; after two bounces, twenty-five. The first one to get to five hundred wins. Okay, line up about thirty yards away or so."

The gang fanned out and got ready to receive Alex's first punt. "I hope you didn't mind my asking Charlie to join us," Gadget said to Chris.

"With him here, how can we have a High-Fives meeting? We've got some very important things to talk about."

"We've got a few things we'd like to talk to you about, too."

"Heads up!" Alex shouted. She held the ball sideways and firmly in her hands with her arms fully extended. Her head was still and her eyes focused on the ball. She stepped with her left foot and dropped her right leg back. In one smooth motion she released the ball, brought her right leg forward, pointed her toe slightly, and let the ball meet her foot just below the ankle on the top side of the arch. It sailed high and long, and the gang scrambled to catch it. Only Charlie had positioned himself far enough in the back to set up for the catch. With very little effort it dropped sweetly into his hands.

"All right, Charlie!" Gadget shouted. "Isn't he the greatest?"

"Terrific," Jack grumbled.

Gadget patted Charlie on the back. "One hundred points."

"It wasn't special," Charlie said, blushing. He passed the ball back to Alex. She caught it, but stumbled back because of the force. It was a perfect spiral.

"Everybody ready?" Alex called after she'd recovered. They all stepped back about ten yards and nodded. Once again she booted a strong kick, this time between Chris and Jack. Both boys ran to catch it. Chris stepped in front of Jack, who tripped on Chris's ankle, sending both of the boys tumbling to the ground. The ball bounced once and J.R. scooped it up.

"Thanks, guys." J.R. was all smiles. "Fifty points."

Jack stood up and brushed the grass from his knees.

"That was my ball. How come you crashed into me like that?"

"Your ball?" Chris shouted back. "In your dreams. It was coming right to me."

"No way."

"Was, too."

"Look, there's an easy solution to this, fellas," Charlie suggested. "Just call for a fair catch. Then if you catch the ball, you get the points, but if it drops, the other guy has the chance to get it."

"Just like in a real game. What a great idea. Isn't he perfect for the High-Fives?" Gadget was beaming.

The gang stood stunned. They couldn't believe Gadget had just said the club name in front of an outsider. Sure they'd used the name High-Fives for their basketball and baseball teams, but this was different, this was personal.

"Gadget!" Chris shouted. "Be careful."

J.R. tossed the ball back and broke the tension. "Okay, from now on we call for a fair catch."

Stretch caught the next one for a hundred points, and Chris and Jack both tallied up a hundred and seventy-five points. Charlie had no trouble racking up three hundred points, getting hundreds every time. Gadget bounced back and forth from the plus to the minus column, and J.R. slowly added up points twenty-five at a time. He usually recovered the ball after Gadget missed it.

"I'm doing something wrong," Gadget groaned.

"You can say that again," Stretch said too loudly.

"I can't seem to get a good grip on the ball."

Jack was sarcastic. "Maybe you ate something bad."

"Or you're not getting enough rest," J.R. added.

"No, I'm in the best physical condition I've ever been in, thanks to Charlie." Gadget rolled up the sleeve of his sweatshirt. "Just feel that bicep, and my triceps and deltoids feel like they're ready to burst. Come on, feel it." He flexed his arm and made a muscle.

J.R. stepped forward. "Nice, very nice," he said blandly.

"I tell you, the new Gadget is even starting to amaze me. Taller, thinner, stronger," Gadget said.

"Dumber," Jack blasted.

"I don't think so, Jack. I doubt if any of my new physical changes have affected my powers of reasoning."

"Maybe just your judgment." Jack walked away. "I'm going to get a drink of water."

"Seriously, guys, if you'd like some help getting into top condition, just ask Charlie. I'm sure he'd be glad to give you some of his secret weapons."

"No, thanks," Chris said.

Stretch shoved his hands in his pockets. "I'll stick with the coaches' workout."

"Come on now, Gadget, they all have their own programs." Charlie shuffled his feet in the grass.

"Well, I wouldn't mind a few pointers on how to get more from a kick," Alex said lightly. "You ever done much kicking in Texas, Palmer?"

Charlie took a few steps closer to Alex. "Well, just

a little bit. I don't know about you, but I find that for punting, if you put your left hand under the far point, and the right hand near the back, you get better spiral action. Plus, hold the ball at a slight angle, so your shoelaces make good contact with the ball." He walked to where Alex was kicking, and the two of them talked strategy.

Chris grabbed the opportunity to talk to Gadget. "What are you doing?"

Gadget looked confused. "What do you mean?"

Stretch joined them. "Look, we know what you and Charlie have been doing in the basement, and we're worried about you."

"You saw us in his basement?"

"We sure did!" J.R. cried.

"Then why didn't you join us?"

Chris hit the palm of his hand on his forehead. "Are you crazy! Do you know what you're saying?"

"It's fun, you'll like it. And the result—well, I'm living proof." Gadget held up his arm to show off his muscle again.

"Don't you know that stuff can kill you?" Jack said, joining the group.

"Not if used properly. It can only make me a better athlete. Look, I realize I don't know that much about it, but Charlie's a real pro, and I trust him."

"Well, we don't," Jack fired back.

"You just don't know him well enough yet."

Stretch kicked at the grass. "I know all I want to know, and I think he's bad news."

"Seriously, you've got to spend more time with him.

That's how I came up with this really terrific idea. I want to ask Charlie to be one of the High-Fives!"

"What?" Chris gasped.

"No way," Stretch added.

Jack stepped back. "Over my dead body."

J.R. looked at Gadget, who was in shock. "Maybe we should discuss it at the next meeting."

"But I thought you'd be thrilled. He's a perfect addition."

Chris tried to reason with him. "Whoever heard of the High-Sixes? It just wouldn't work."

"The club is full." Jack started pacing. "Besides, we don't have any fingers left on our High-Five hand."

"Don't you realize we don't need one? It's perfect already. His last name already fits. *Palm*-er—you know, like the palm of your hand. It's fate. It's the core of our secret handshake, the palm."

"Oh, it's the core all right," Stretch groaned. "A rotten apple core."

Chris agreed. "Forget it, Gadget. It won't work."

"We're not interested," Jack added.

Gadget stood firm with his hands on his hips. "Well then, maybe I'm not interested, either. Come on, Charlie," he called to his new friend. "Let's go to your house. I need another dose of the Palmer secret weapon. I think we've been kicked around enough for one day."

Chapter 11

FATE'S MIS-FORTUNE

"Did Gadget talk to you during calisthenics?" Chris asked the next day before their scrimmage.

"Me?" Jack shrugged. "I'd be the last person he'd talk to. He's maddest at me."

J.R. made a pile of towels on the edge of the bench. "He doesn't understand the trouble he's in, or that we want to help."

"It's the drugs, I tell ya." Stretch shook his head. "He's not thinking straight because of the drugs."

"I still can hardly believe it," J.R. stated. He handed out helmets and pads to the gang.

Jack hit his head with the palm of his hand. "What more proof do you need? Wasn't the library enough? Just look at Gadget. Can't you at least believe your eyes?"

"It's just like the books said: His arms are bigger, his voice is lower, he's bulkier." Stretch straightened his shoulder pads.

Jack pulled on his gold T-shirt. "He does seem quicker than he's ever been."

"I just wish he knew that taking steroids is the beginning of the end," Chris added, pulling a helmet on his head.

"Yeah, the more you take them, the bigger the bad side effects. Heart problems, you stop growing, that weird Frankenstein thing that makes you look like a gorilla." Stretch made a face like a monkey.

"Oh, you mean like Charlie," Jack added.

"They can kill you."

"Here you go again saying Gadget's going to die."

"Don't worry, J.R., we're not going to let him," Chris said.

J.R. slapped a helmet. "We've got to stop him and that's that."

"It's the source we've got to stop," Stretch said, pointing to Charlie.

"I guess there's no hope that Charlie will be cut from the team today, huh?"

Chris rolled his eyes. "Right."

Jack's eyes brightened. "Yeah, but maybe Gadget will."

"That's a terrible thing to say," J.R. snapped.

"It would solve the problem."

"Not if he's really hooked."

Chris slumped onto the bench. "You're right. We'll probably be cut before Gadget. If we don't do anything spectacular on the field today, our places on the squad will be on the line."

*　　*　　*

"Don't you want to go over some of the other plays with your friends?" Charlie asked as he took a handoff from Gadget and dashed forward.

Gadget glanced at the High-Fives. "I'm working with *my* friend. Come on, let's try the Quarterback Sneak."

Charlie centered the ball. "On four, right?"

"Correct," Gadget replied, shifting his weight. "Sly Fox!" he shouted to the pretend line. "Hut one, hut two." Charlie snapped the ball to Gadget. He tucked the ball low and into his stomach, hunching over it for protection. With his head down he pretended to run in for a touchdown.

"Six points!" Charlie shouted. "You'll be a hero."

"I just hope I'm not cut from the team."

"Not the Mustangs' star quarterback."

Gadget blushed. "I'm not the star. I'm not even the only quarterback. Kevin McClarnon seems to be connecting with all the pass plays. I've got to get better on the pass."

"Did you drink your super-duper power potion this morning?"

"Yes," Gadget said halfheartedly. "And I took the pills, too. I'm just not sure they're going to make a difference. The medical community hasn't proved their effectiveness."

"Just look at your biceps and tell me they're not effective."

Gadget flexed his muscles and smiled.

Prrt! Prrt! Prrrt! Coach Halligan blew his whistle sharply, calling the team together. "I want you to play your best today. It may be your last chance to show me what you can do. Again, I remind you, I'm not looking for perfection, but I will be looking for determination and an all-out effort.''

Gadget clenched his fists. "That's what I'll do."

"Coach Bozeman will talk to the defense, and I want to go over the play sequence with the offense, then we'll get on with the game."

Gadget glanced at the High-Fives as they joined the rest of the offensive team. He couldn't understand why they were being so pigheaded. Charlie was a terrific guy. He would make a great member of the High-Fives. They just didn't know him as well as he did. He promised himself to get each of them to spend time with Charlie. Then it would only be a matter of time until the whole gang agreed he'd be the perfect High-Five. He listened to Coach Halligan and memorized each new play.

That day's scrimmage was going to be the toughest, Gadget thought. It was going to take a real team effort, and that was going to be hard since he wasn't even talking to most of the offensive squad. He wasn't mad at them, just confused by them. He couldn't pinpoint why they resented Charlie. Charlie said they might be jealous because he was playing quarterback, or that he had grown taller and thinner. It could even be the contact lenses. But that didn't sound like the High-Fives he knew. He slipped his helmet on and decided it wasn't the day for fighting. He'd set aside any anger for the scrimmage, and then he'd convince his friends to listen to reason.

Coach Halligan's whistle sounded the start of the scrimmage. Alex's kickoff was solid, and Mike took it at the twenty-yard line, running up the sideline until the Raider pack brought him down at the twenty-four. "Offense on the field, and let's hustle."

Gadget bolted onto the field and huddled at the twenty-two. The High-Fives had their heads down as they listened. "The play sequence is one, two, and then eight. One is Red Bullet four."

Jack raised his head and smiled. Red Bullet was a pass play to him ten yards down. "First down, here we come."

"That's right," Gadget said, staring into his eyes. "Today more than ever it's all for one and one for all." The team looked at one another, but it was the High-Fives that Gadget made sure the message got to. He wished J.R. was there, too. "On four." Gadget clapped, and the offense sprung to their three-point stance on the twenty-four.

"Bye-bye, High-Fives," Randy said through gritted teeth.

"We're going to get rid of all of you today," Greg added.

"Cut city," Hank slobbered through his mouth guard.

Gadget blocked out their voices and concentrated on the play. "Red Bullet four!" he shouted to the right side of the line. "Red Bullet four!" he repeated to the left. "Hut one, hut two." The ball smacked into his hands, and he dropped back. The defensive line came at him full force, and Gadget quickly scrambled right

100

to avoid the biggest mass. For an instant he could see Jack running in the clear, ten yards down. He darted around Hank and fired the ball. For once his aim was right on, and the last thing he saw was Jack leaping up to catch it successfully before he felt a sharp pain in his side and crashed to the ground.

"Eat dirt, Shaw," Randy grumbled before jumping off Gadget.

The whistle blew the play dead, and Gadget pulled himself up to peer downfield. "Did he hold on to it?"

Chris ran back all smiles. "First down with two yards to spare."

"Bull's-eye," Stretch added.

Jack high-fived Gadget. "Now, that's what I call teamwork."

For the moment all the problems between the gang melted away. They were a team again, and Gadget let out a deep sigh of relief. They huddled up.

Alex ran in. "Coach says good work." She gave Gadget a punch on the shoulder. "Continue with the sequence, and I'll be back in two downs."

Gadget nodded. "That takes us to Pied Piper one. Okay, Charlie, show us your stuff. I'll hand off to you, and you won't need to stop until you're over the end zone." The team clapped and set up for the play. It was a smooth handoff, and Charlie gained nine yards, just leaving them short of another first down.

"He really is good," Stretch said as he walked with Chris back to the line of scrimmage.

"Yeah, too bad he's crooked."

The team enthusiastically huddled again. "This feels

great. The coach can't cut us if we're winning." Chris grinned.

"So let's keep going," Jack added. "Baby Boomer four is next."

"You ready, Jack?" Gadget asked. "I'll hand off to you, so get us that yard."

"It's a done deal."

The snap from the center came a little shaky, and Gadget bobbled the handoff to Jack. If it hadn't been for Charlie's quick thinking, the offense would have been thrown for a loss. Instead, he plowed in front of Gadget and made the opening large enough for Jack to stumble the yard.

"I want a measurement," Ron Porter demanded.

"This is just a scrimmage, son," Coach Bozeman said as he placed the ball on the forty-six-yard line.

"The pros would get a measurement."

"The pros wouldn't have let him get the yard." Coach Bozeman blew his whistle.

"You guys look really strong today," Alex said as she brought in the next sequence of plays.

"That's one way to put it." Charlie smiled, nudging Gadget.

Chris looked at Jack, and the thought of steroids flooded back into the picture. "We've got a long way to go before we make it over that end zone."

"So do it," Alex said. "Coach says four, then ten followed by three. See you for the extra point."

Four was Paul's Dodge City six, and for the first time all week Gadget was able to complete the fifteen-yard pass to him for another first down.

"We're in enemy territory," Charlie said, congratulating Gadget. "The thirty-nine-yard line."

"Okay, it's time for a new play." Gadget called the huddle closer. "This is Porch Door three, the screen play to Stretch. We haven't practiced it much, so stay on top of it." The huddle broke, and Gadget knew he was nervous as he stepped behind the center. By the time he was calling the hut sequence, his voice was cracking with each number. The snap came sharp.

Gadget dropped back into the pocket. It was terrifying to see the whole defensive line pushing its way to massacre him for a loss. It was like the whole offensive line had fallen apart. Gadget turned to the right, looked over the defense, and dumped the ball into the flat. The offensive line had followed their orders perfectly and created a wall for Stretch, who had no problem advancing to the thirty, a yard short of another first down.

"What a drive!" Chris cheered.

"You were terrific, Gadget," Stretch said, giving him a high-five. For a moment the old gang acted like the old gang, jumping in the air and slapping hands. Even J.R. cheered from the sidelines.

Gadget was all smiles in the huddle. "All right, Chris, it's time for the draw play, Yellow Jacket three."

"Just remember who we're trying to fake."

"It'll be in your hands before you know it."

The huddle broke and the offense went into action. Gadget dropped back, faked the handoff to Charlie, quickly reversed, and placed it in Chris's hands. Chris darted around Greg, and then Ron chased him three more yards before he pulled him down hard. The offense was on the twenty-one. First and ten.

"Number nine, Topsy-Turvy." Alex darted in and out of the huddle to keep the pace moving.

Gadget sighed, a little relieved. Topsy-Turvy didn't depend on Gadget having a great throwing arm—that was Charlie's job. Gadget would lateral to the fullback, who passed to Stretch for the touchdown. Once again everybody took his job seriously, and even though Charlie had to scramble for the lateral, he played like a pro with his strong arm and direct aim. Stretch stumbled as he caught the direct hit but recovered immediately.

"All the way," Gadget mumbled.

Stretch kicked into high gear and pushed past Greg and Hank as if they were snails. He high-stepped around Randy at the ten-yard line and focused on the end zone. Suddenly Ron darted in from nowhere and brought Stretch to the ground on the two-yard line as if he were a rag doll. The High-Fives went wild.

"What a run!"

"Charlie's pass was perfection," Gadget cheered.

"Stretch's moves weren't too shabby, either."

Charlie slapped Gadget's back. "Now it's touch-down time."

"We haven't made it yet," Jack cautioned.

"And you're not going to, either!" Ron shouted across the line of scrimmage.

"Yeah, well, I'd like to see you try to stop us," Stretch added, still shaken a bit from the hard tackle.

Chris helped Stretch up. "You haven't stopped us yet."

"Well, your luck is about to run out," Greg barked back.

Coach Bozeman ran over to the group and broke up what could become a fight. "Watch it, boys, or you'll be watching the rest of the game from the bench—or the locker room." Both sides grumbled but jogged to their respective huddles.

Alex ran in with Coach Halligan's instructions. "Sly Fox."

"It's the Quarterback Sneak. We've never done it before." Gadget was scared. "Maybe Charlie should do a running play."

"No, the coach is right," Charlie insisted. "Great time to fake out the biggest fakers of them all."

"I don't know, guys," Gadget said, shaking his head.

Jack grabbed his shoulders. "Look, we're on the two-yard line. All you have to do is fall over it."

Chris agreed. "Besides, if you tell the coach you don't want to do the play, he'll think you're chicken."

"And maybe cut you from the squad," Stretch added.

"I guess, but you've got to help me."

"We'll be right behind you," Charlie said with a smile. "If I have to, I'll pick you up and toss you over myself."

"You may have to." Gadget jumped when Coach Bozeman blew the warning whistle.

Gadget could feel his hands sweating as he lined up

behind the center. He hoped he wouldn't fumble the ball. He cleared his throat and glanced over his shoulder, nodding to Charlie. He wondered if he really would toss him over the end zone. Gadget wished Charlie were the quarterback. "Sly Fox one," he called to the right. "Sly Fox one," he repeated to the left. "Hut one." The ball practically jammed his fingers. Without thinking Gadget leaped into the air. He knew he'd have to go high as well as far. There was a small pocket, and he twisted his body forward to glide through it. Suddenly he felt a sharp pain in his left ankle. At the same time a dull shock ran through his shoulder. He fell to the ground and lay still, taking inventory of all of his bones and muscles. For a minute he didn't even hear the offense screaming touchdown.

"You were fantastic," Chris said, kneeling beside Gadget.

"Just like a pro," Charlie added.

Gadget slowly pushed up onto his elbow and started to get up. Then he fell back in shock. "I can't move my leg!"

Chapter 12

EMERGENCY

"I can't get Gadget's face out of my mind." Chris wiped his sweaty forehead with his sleeve.

"He looked so scared when they carried him off the field," Jack added.

Stretch stepped on the ribbed rubber mat that led to the entrance of Conrad General's emergency room. "I hate hospitals." The doors slid open.

Chris pointed to the emergency room arrow on the wall. "I'm glad Coach Halligan let J.R. go with him."

"Yeah. It killed me to have to stay," Jack added.

Stretch rounded the first corner. "At least both his folks were on duty. I guess he's lucky they're both doctors."

"I just hope he's all right."

"He will be."

"He's got to be." Chris sighed. "It makes me feel weird about all that drug stuff that happened yesterday."

Jack stopped dead in his tracks. "Oh, no, this could get very sticky."

"What do you mean, sticky?" Stretch asked.

"Don't quote me, but don't they take a blood sample and run all sorts of tests when you go to the hospital?"

Stretch shrugged. "Yeah, so?"

"So if the doctors check his blood, they're going to know that he's on steroids."

The boys picked up their pace following the signs to the emergency room. "Do you think J.R. could protect him?"

"Probably not, but maybe he could talk to him." Stretch shook his head. "Man, this whole thing is messy."

Chris stopped the others before they went to the nurses' station to find out where Gadget was. "Look, the most important thing right now is to let Gadget know that we're his friends."

"Agreed." Jack nodded. "Hey, there's J.R."

The gang jogged past the nurse to where J.R. was sitting in a small waiting room with his chin resting in his hands.

"Where's Gadget?" Jack asked.

Chris sat next to the younger Klipp. "How is he?"

"He's okay, kinda banged up. He's in that room with his folks. They made me come out here and wait until they were finished with some tests."

"Oh, no," Jack gasped. "What kind of tests?"

J.R. shrugged. "I'm not sure. They gave him a shot."

"Ah, geez, I hate needles." Stretch cringed.

Jack grabbed his brother's arm. "Did they take any blood?"

"Or make him give them a urine sample?" Chris added.

"No, I don't think so. Why would they do that? He hurt his ankle."

Jack spun around. "Maybe they made J.R. leave 'cause they found out about the drugs from the tests."

Chris pulled Jack down on the couch by him. "We've got to stay calm until we know for sure. Remember, we're here as Gadget's friends."

"This whole thing makes me nervous," Stretch added.

"That's why we have to keep our eyes open and our mouths shut." Chris looked over his shoulder to make sure no one else was listening. "Okay?"

"Okay," the others whispered back.

"You can come back in now," Gadget's dad said, cracking the door to a small examining room. The High-Fives flinched at the sound of his voice. "Oh, hi, fellas. Why don't you all come in? I'm sure Gadget would like to see you."

They all jumped up, with J.R. leading the way back into the room. "Hey, hero, how's it going?" He tried to smile.

"Not too good," Gadget said, trying to smile back. He was lying on a silver gurney with three pillows piled behind his head and another stack underneath his left leg. There were ice packs surrounding his ankle, which was in a cast of plastic and Velcro. He was wearing his glasses and holding a pillow. His gold T-shirt and shoulder pads sat on a chair.

"Is it busted?" Stretch asked quietly.

"No, it's the ligaments. Looks like my quarter-backing days are over." Gadget swallowed the lump in his throat.

"At least for this season." Gadget's mom handed her son a glass of juice. "Maybe only six to eight weeks."

"The coach will have cut me long before that." Gadget struggled to hold back the tears.

"I don't think so," Chris said. "He posted the cut list before we left, and your name wasn't on it."

"Really? At least I know I didn't blow it so far."

"Are you kidding?" Stretch said, leaping into action. "You were amazing today. Passing, running—you did it all."

"That is, until I got hit by a brick wall."

"Well, that's Ron Porter for ya," Jack muttered.

"But we showed him the High-Fives couldn't be pushed around." Stretch strutted around the room.

"No, just broken in two." Gadget chuckled, trying to hide his pain. "Hey, how about you guys? None of you were cut, were you?"

Chris held his hand in the air. "All for one and one for all."

"What about Charlie?"

Jack wanted to say something snide but held it back. "What do you think? The coach would be crazy to cut him."

"I was hoping he might be with you."

"Coach asked him to stay after for a minute, or I'm sure he would have come," Chris reassured him.

"Mom, Dad, do you think I could talk to my friends alone for a few minutes before we go home?"

"Sure, son," Gadget's mom said. "We'll go finish signing the papers and come back."

"Thanks, Mom." Gadget watched them until they walked out of the room. "Have you guys given any more thought to asking Charlie to join the club?"

The others exchanged looks.

"Now more than ever I think it's important. I'm not going to be able to pull my weight on the squad, and Charlie is perfect. He can be all the things I never could be and more."

J.R. sighed. "We like you just the way you are."

"You sound like we want to replace you just 'cause you got banged up." Chris sat in a chair.

"It's important to me, really."

"Maybe we can discuss it at the next meeting," Jack mumbled.

"He's perfect, guys. His name fits and everything— it's fate. You just need to get to know him like I do. I can't tell you the things he's done for me."

"I wouldn't be too sure about that," Stretch whispered to Chris.

"Please, guys, please."

"We'll talk about it when you feel better." J.R. patted Gadget's arm.

"All right, son." Gadget's dad came back into the room. "We've got your crutches in the car, so as soon as the wheelchair shows up, we'll head home."

Chris was the first one to reach the door. "We'll come over and see you tomorrow."

"Yeah, take care of yourself." Stretch slid out.

"Tell the coach I'm okay."

"Will do," Jack added as the door closed. The gang walked silently over to the couch and chairs in the waiting room.

"So what are we going to do?" Chris asked.

J.R. took a deep breath. "I think if including Charlie is that important to Gadget, we should think about it."

"But it's wrong, all wrong."

Stretch agreed. "Jack's right, we can't ask a druggie to join our secret club."

"We don't know he's on drugs for sure," J.R. fired back.

"Well, then, we'd better find out and quick," Chris suggested.

"We need to get evidence, samples of the pills and potion." Chris was serious. "Then we don't need to ask Gadget—we can go right to Charlie. If he's innocent, then maybe we could ask him to join the club."

J.R. nodded. "I think if we ask Charlie to join, we should ask Alex, too."

"What?" Jack gasped.

"She's been with us from the start."

Jack stood up. "She's a girl. This whole thing is totally out of hand. The High-Fives are falling apart. All for none and none for all is more like it." He flipped his jacket over his shoulder and stormed out.

112

Chapter 13

TWO BIRDS WITH ONE STONE

"Hi, Gadget, how are you feeling day?" J.R. poked his head into Gadget's bedroom.

"Physically or emotionally?" Gadget answered glumly.

J.R. pulled up the chair from Gadget's desk and set it next to the bed. "Is there a difference?"

"Colossal. Just between you and me, I think my ankle feels better than my brain."

"You got a headache?"

Gadget grinned. "No, J.R., I'm depressed."

"How come?"

Gadget pushed himself up higher in bed. "I've been stuck in this bed for the whole week, and I'm going crazy. You may not believe this, but I haven't touched my computer in three days. Now, the old Gadget wouldn't have cared whether he was stuck inside all week or not—actually, he'd have loved it. Everything he needed right at his fingertips. But not the new Gadget. J.R., I feel so different. All I can think about is football. Passes, draw plays, blitzes, screens. I wish I could jump up and run the obstacle course a zillion times."

"Don't tell that to the other guys. Chris is ready to take a jackhammer to the blocking sleds."

"I'd give away my physics and zoology programs for one afternoon in Charlie's basement. I really miss my workouts. I can feel my muscles withering by the hour. I'd really started to notice a difference, too, didn't you?"

J.R. shrugged. "Kinda. Look, maybe all that stuff Charlie was showing you wasn't that good for you."

"I want to share a secret with you." Gadget pulled open the top drawer of his nightstand. "This is Charlie's secret weapon." He held up three small plastic bags filled with pills. One was filled with dark red oval-shaped ones. Another had capsules half green and half yellow. The last one held tiny circular white pills. "These plus some of this power potion have changed my life." He took the lid off a metal thermos and poured the famous thick beige liquid into a cup. "It takes a while to get used to the taste, but in a few days you almost like it. Here, try some."

J.R. trembled as Gadget handed him the cup. "No, thanks, I just had lunch. Maybe later. What are those supposed to do?" J.R. asked, nervously pointing to the pills. He had a plan. He'd show the rest of the High-Fives once and for all that they were wrong about Gadget, Charlie, and the steroids. If he could get a sample of this junk and have it tested, he could prove that he was right. "Do you take these pills every day?"

"Yes, one red, one green-and-yellow, and a couple of the small white ones. It depends on the workout. You want some? I'm sure Charlie wouldn't mind." He handed a day's supply to J.R.

"I'll take them with the power potion—later."

"So tell me about practice. When the other guys visit, they feel like they can't talk about it, but you'll tell me everything. Please, J.R., tell me everything."

J.R. could see the desperate look in his best friend's eyes. "I'll tell you what I know." Both boys relaxed and smiled. "Well, first off, Coach Halligan did the second cut today. All the High-Fives, the Raiders, Alex, and Charlie are still on the team."

"All the High-Fives?"

"Just like Coach Halligan said. He won't cut you from the squad until he feels it's absolutely necessary. I think he's waiting for the doctor's final decision."

"I'm not even supposed to put weight on my foot until Monday. Then I'll be on crutches for weeks." Gadget laid his head back on the pillows. "I'll do anything. I can't be cut from the team."

"Remember when I thought I didn't have a chance to be a part of the Mustangs?"

"Sure."

"And how you wouldn't let me give up."

"This is different."

"No, it's not, Gadget. This time *I've* got an idea,

and *you're* going to have to trust me. You said you'll be outside on your crutches on Monday, right?''

"Wild horses couldn't stop me."

"Okay, then meet me by the big tree in the park across from Mike's Diner at noon."

"I don't know, J.R."

"Come on, Gadget, you said you'd do anything."

Gadget smiled. "I did say that, didn't I?"

J.R. stood up. "Yep, you sure did." J.R. tucked the pills in his pocket and held the cup half hidden in his hand. "I gotta go. Cheer up, and I'll see you Monday, okay?"

"Affirmative, and, J.R.—thanks."

J.R. opened the door. "Where are your contacts?"

Gadget shrugged. "I don't know, I kind of missed my glasses. I kept pushing them up on my nose anyway."

J.R. closed the door and clutched the pills in his pocket. For a moment he wanted to call the guys and tell them he had the evidence they needed to prove Gadget's innocence. He stopped on the front step to think. He looked up at Gadget's window and had second thoughts. The gang wanted to prove him guilty, so he was going to have to find a way to do this on his own. He couldn't walk up to the hospital lab or the police station and say, "Will you test these?" They'd ask too many questions. He didn't think Gadget was guilty, but he had to be sure. J.R. sighed and sat on the curb next to his bike. Gadget would know what to do, he thought. Suddenly he had an answer. He folded the corners of the paper cup to keep the potion from spilling, hopped on his bike, and headed home.

"Hi, honey, what's up?" Mrs. Klipp's soft voice greeted J.R. in the kitchen. She was a short woman with soft brown eyes, and angular features. Her dark hair was twisted in a knot on top of her head, and she was sipping a cup of coffee at the table.

"Can I talk to you?"

"Of course you can."

"It's serious, Mom. I can't tell you much, and I'm sure you'll have lots of questions, but I can't give you many answers. What I can say is that it has nothing to do with Jack or me."

Mrs. Klipp touched J.R.'s hand. "This is serious."

"Probably the most serious thing I've ever done. Are you still friends with Mrs. Chase, the nurse?"

"Yes, why?"

J.R. laid the pills on the table and set the cup next to them. "Could you ask her to test these?"

"Where did you get them?"

"I can't tell you, Mom. At least, not yet. I promise if they're something bad, I'll tell you anything you want to know."

J.R.'s mom took a deep breath. "You boys are growing up so fast. I'll talk to Carol—Mrs. Chase—and if she can help out, I'm sure she will."

"Thanks, Mom, it's really important. It could be a matter of life and death." J.R. got up from the table. "I've got to go call the guys."

Chapter 14

THE FINAL CUT

"Hey, where's that kid brother of yours?" Ron Porter shouted at Jack. "How am I suppose to get my equipment if the equipment manager isn't here?"

Jack put his foot up on the bench and retied his shoe. "Keep your shirt on, Porter, he's probably helping the coach type up the final cut sheet. I hear your name's at the top."

"Think again, Klipp. It's going to be that four-eyed faker Gadget Shaw. He hasn't worked out with the team for two weeks."

Chris intervened. "If you hadn't clobbered him so hard, he'd still be here."

"Hey, if he can't take it, then he shouldn't be on the team, anyway." Ron walked toward the blocking sleds and the rest of the Raiders.

Stretch squinted as he tried to look toward the gym to see if J.R. was in sight. "It isn't like J.R. to be late."

"Mom was supposed to get the test results back on those drug samples today," said Jack. "He was determined to get them before practice."

Chris plopped down on the grass. "Man, as if today isn't tense enough, we have to deal with that stuff, too."

"J.R. said Gadget was coming today."

"To do what? Hobble around the field a couple of times? Coach Halligan can't hold on to him any longer if he isn't doing anything for the team." Jack did some toe touches.

"It's going to kill him," Chris added.

Stretch agreed. "I don't think J.R.'s going to take it very well, either."

"J.R. hasn't told him about Charlie, either, I bet."

Chris joined Jack in leg stretches. "You mean that he's the quarterback now? I doubt it."

"Actually, I don't think Gadget would mind," Jack grumbled. "He still thinks Charlie's the ultimate athlete."

"I hope we get those test results back today," Chris added. "The suspense is killing me."

"What's killing me is whether I'll make this team." Stretch ran in place.

"Right now I'm more worried about J.R. not showing up. He could be in big trouble if he blows it today."

"I'm going inside to give my mom a call," Jack said, throwing down a towel.

"Stretch and I'll hand out the equipment. If Coach

Halligan comes out and sees that no one is suited up, we'll all be in hot water."

The gang jumped into action long enough to see J.R., Alex, and Gadget coming out of the gym with Coach Halligan. Chris ran full steam ahead to meet them. "Hey, it's great to see you outside again."

"And vertical," Gadget added. "I was starting to feel like I was nailed to my bed."

"J.R., you've got a lot of work to do." Coach Halligan sounded stern. "We start the scrimmage in ten minutes." The gang scrambled in all directions, leaving Gadget to hobble to the sidelines bench on his own.

"Did you get the results?" Jack asked his brother.

"Nothing yet. Gadget and I were talking to the coach, but Mom says she'll bring them over as soon as she gets them."

The next few minutes were crazy as everyone nervously picked up their helmets, pads, and shirts. Even the Raiders weren't as cocky as they usually were. "I guess today is do-or-die day for the Dugan Mustangs," Chris said, panting after a quick sprint.

"More than that," Jack added. "It's do-or-die day for the High-Fives."

Coach Halligan blew his whistle, and the squad converged at the sidelines bench. "I know everyone is tense about today's scrimmage, but this is only half the tension you'll feel at a real game. Try to relax and use that energy to play better ball. You're a great group of guys—oh, and gal—and I want you to know you've made my job of selection very difficult. You know what to do—now get out there and do it." The team gathered around the coach, and like a group of ants scrambling to the center of an anthill, they piled their hands in a mound. Even Gadget managed to hop over to the outside and be a part of the action. "All for one and one for all!" they shouted in unison.

Gadget took a deep breath. "Go get 'em, offense." The High-Fives all waved or gave him the thumbs-up sign as they plopped on their helmets and waited for Alex and the special team to set up. A long kick to the seventeen, with a run back by Mike, put the action into full force. The offense took over at the twenty-seven. "I think I'm more nervous for the team sitting on the sidelines," Gadget said.

J.R. nodded his head. "Now you know how I've felt the past three weeks. If an eleven-year-old could turn gray, I think I'd be an old man by now."

"So do you wish you were out there with them?" Alex said as she took off her helmet and sat on the other side of Gadget.

Gadget cocked his head. "Yes, I do. Who would have ever believed that brainy Gadget Shaw wanted to be in the middle of a football tackle?"

"You'll be back," J.R. said encouragingly.

Suddenly the conversation stopped, and Gadget looked on the field. "Charlie's the quarterback."

"We wanted to tell you," J.R. started.

"We just didn't know how you'd feel," Alex added.

Gadget could feel his heart pounding harder in his chest. He had known he'd be replaced, and he'd wanted to ask a jillion times who it was when the gang

121

came to visit him, but he'd never imagined Charlie in his spot. It had always been some faceless kid that he didn't even know.

Alex spoke softly. "When the coach saw how he could pass a ball on the Topsy-Turvy play, he reassigned him."

"That's great," Gadget mumbled. Slowly a smile crossed his face. "That really is great," he added with a full grin. "Charlie's perfect. I don't know why it didn't dawn on me earlier."

"We hoped you wouldn't be upset."

"J.R., I'd be a little upset no matter who it was. This way's the best because it's a friend."

"I knew you'd feel that way." Alex flipped her long blond braid over her shoulder.

"Hey, they're about to start the sequence. Let me see if I can guess what plays they're going to use." He closed his eyes and thought back to the blue spiral notebook. "Dodge City, Tinhorn, and then maybe Screaming Eagle."

"Could be," Alex said. "I gotta go stand by the coach to run in plays. Talk to you later."

The offense positioned themselves on the line of scrimmage. Gadget thought that Charlie looked so strong and confident in the center of the pack. Gadget couldn't make out the call, but as soon as the ball was snapped, he knew the play. It was Paul's pass play, Dodge City, and it resulted in a gain of five.

"Way to go, offense!" Gadget cheered through cupped hands.

The huddle was fast, and it didn't take Gadget long

to figure out that the handoff would go to Chris. He twisted through a small hole the linesman had created for a gain of three. It was third down and two on the thirty-five.

"If I were in there, I'd give the ball to Charlie for a running play. Who's the new fullback?"

"A guy named Craig. He's good, and a nice guy, too. You'll like him."

The offense lined up again. "I'll bet the defense goes for the blitz," Gadget said, figuring the odds.

"They don't have much of a choice, but Charlie's a tough one to tackle. He's only been sacked once since he took over." J.R. covered his mouth, feeling self-conscious. "Sorry."

Gadget nudged him lightly. "It's okay, J.R. I have no doubts that Charlie is a stronger quarterback. You don't have to apologize. I think my math scores are probably better than his. It's an even exchange."

When they looked back on the field, they saw Stretch barreling downfield for a long pass. "It's the Screaming Eagle. Run, Evans, run!" J.R. sprang to his feet.

Gadget forgot about his ankle and tried to do the same. He grabbed J.R.'s shoulder in time to keep from falling. Stretch caught the ball despite the fact that Ron had pushed him. "Interference!" Gadget shouted.

Stretch stumbled the next few yards and finally fell out of bounds on the defense forty-two. "All right!" J.R. cheered.

"First down," Gadget added.

Despite the penalty and the great run, the next

sequence of plays brought little progress from the offense. Randy had stopped Chris short on the line of scrimmage. Stretch completed a small screen play for two yards, but Greg Forbes had almost intercepted. It was third and six, and the offense needed a play.

"What do you think they'll do?" J.R. asked.

"I'm not sure," Gadget answered, deep in thought. "They could try to plow through with Craig, but they'll be expecting that. Maybe Yellow Jacket, the fake handoff to Chris. If I were coaching, I think I'd try the Quarterback Sneak."

"Really?"

"Of course. Why not? Charlie was a great fullback. He'd be perfect to pull it off." A moment later they had their answer. Gadget had outguessed the coach, and Charlie hurled forward to try for the first down. As soon as it looked as if he might make the break, the Raiders pulled him down two yards short.

"Darn," J.R. grumbled. "And it was such a good drive. Do you think they'll go for it?"

"I doubt it—too risky and too early in the game."

Suddenly a shadow blocked the boys' view. "Do you think you're ready?" Alex had her helmet on, ready to kick. "Coach wants to try a field goal."

"Really." Gadget practically sprung to his feet. "I'm ready, really ready."

"Do you want some help out onto the field?" J.R. asked.

"I would, but I'd better not. If I'm going to make the final cut, I'd better be able to prove to the coach and the team that I deserve it."

Alex flung her arm under Gadget's shoulder for a little support, and the two of them walked cautiously onto the field. "Just take it easy, relax, and we'll do it just like we practiced in the park with J.R."

"Hey, look," Chris called. "What's Gadget doing on the field with Alex?"

The special teams exchanged places with the offense, and Gadget lowered himself onto the grass. He knelt with most of his weight on his good leg, while he tucked the leg in the cast behind him with a little weight on his knee for balance. "Okay, this is it," Gadget mumbled to himself. "If you want to make the squad, you've got to do your job."

Jack grabbed his little brother off the bench. "You know what's going on out there, don't you?"

"Sure do. Since Doug got cut from the team last week, you've seen what happens when Alex goes for the extra point or a field goal. Half the time she doesn't even get a chance to try, because the holder keeps messing up the snap from center."

"That's for sure. Peter Farrell is the worst."

"So Alex and Gadget and I worked all week to see how he is at holding. He hasn't missed one yet."

The whistle blew. The snap and the defensive rush seemed to happen simultaneously. The ball came high, but Gadget shot his arms up and snatched it into himself. He could sense the stampede of players coming his way, but he stayed calm and controlled as he twisted the laces toward Alex. He placed the ball at an angle and set his finger on top. In a matter of seconds Alex's swift kick met the pigskin and sent it soaring through the uprights. Gadget sighed a sigh of relief. He'd done his job, and it resulted in three points for the team.

Alex was the first to congratulate him. "Perfect, perfect, perfect. I haven't been able to kick like that since the first week of practice. Thanks!"

J.R. helped Gadget up. "You were great. How'd it feel?"

"It's a lot harder than it looks. The toughest part is ignoring all the guys running in for the kill."

"Well, you did it," Chris cheered.

Stretch helped Gadget to the sidelines. "You've been holding out on us, you little sneak."

"Yeah, puts new meaning into the Quarterback Sneak," Jack added.

"Well, I'm not the quarterback anymore—Charlie is. And he's doing a great job."

Charlie blushed. "I'd still trade you to be your fullback."

The rest of the scrimmage went well. Alex had three more chances to kick. One for another field goal and two for extra points. Gadget held for all of them, and they were all successes. Coach Halligan blew his whistle, and the squad came over to the sidelines. "That's it for today. Hit the showers, and I'll have the final team list posted on my office door before you leave. I want to congratulate you. You've met your challenges, and I'd be proud to work with all of you."

Gadget could feel something in the pit of his stomach grow like a volcano about to erupt. He knew he'd done his best. He just hoped it would be enough.

"Hey, J.R., isn't that your mom coming across the field?"

"Yeah, it is," Jack answered, tapping his brother on the shoulder. "Come on, J.R., we'd better see what she wants." The two Klipp brothers bolted across the field while Stretch and Chris helped Gadget back to the gym.

"Where's Charlie?" Gadget twisted around to find his new friend.

"Last I saw him, he was talking to some strange man over by the bleachers." Chris pointed to Charlie and a large man in a cowboy hat. Charlie didn't look happy.

"Do you think we should ask him if he's okay?"

"Nah," Alex said, joining the group. "I heard the coach talking to him earlier. It must be someone Charlie knows."

"Probably his supplier," Stretch mumbled.

The team filed into the locker room. Alex slipped into the girls'. Gadget headed immediately for the showers, while Jack motioned for Stretch and Chris to meet him and J.R. behind one of the last rows of lockers. The guys made sure that Gadget didn't see them as they sneaked into the corner.

"So spill it," Stretch said.

Chris grabbed for the paper. "What does the hospital say?"

"Are we going to have to go to the police?"

J.R. held the results tightly in his hands. "No, none of the above. You were all wrong. Wrong about Charlie, and most of all, wrong about Gadget." He revealed

127

the first page on the document. "Mom says it's all in here, solid proof. Read it."

Jack's voice hinted of embarrassment. "The red pills were multivitamins, the green-and-yellows were vitamin B complex, and the all-important little white pills were salt tablets."

"That's why he took one of each colored pill, they were vitamins," J.R. said with a smile. "And the number of salt tablets depended on how hot it was and how tough the workout was."

"What about the beige liquid?" Chris asked.

"That's the best one yet," J.R. gloated. "It's desiccated liver, wheat germ, protein powder, and a little honey."

"No steroids?"

"None, zipp-o."

Stretch scratched his head. "Then how did he get so big so fast?"

"By working out." Gadget's voice boomed off the lockers at the end of the row as he stood still wet from his shower. "You thought Charlie was giving me steroids?"

Chris lowered his head. "It sort of looked that way."

"And we were worried about you," Chris added.

"So that's why you were all acting so strangely. And why you didn't want to give Charlie a chance."

"Not to mention asking him into the club," Jack added.

"Well, why didn't you just ask me?"

"We were afraid. You were so strong on Charlie, we wanted to check it out ourselves."

"I can't believe you thought I'd ever take drugs. What kind of a dope do you think I am? I had the vitamins checked out, since I wasn't sure I should even be taking those. You should have asked me. You guys forgot to take into account that I'm working out with weights, growing taller, thinner, and even my voice is starting to change." Gadget shook his head. "Drugs—no way, never."

J.R. crossed his arms over his chest. "We should have trusted you, but football was awfully important to you. You said so yourself."

"But that stuff can kill you."

"We know," Chris said. "And we didn't want to lose you."

The gang was silent for a minute, and then they all held up their hands for the High-Five secret slap. For the first time in three weeks the gang felt like a group again.

"The list is up!" Ron Porter's voice bounced off the walls.

The gang held their grasp for a second. "No matter what happens, we're still the High-Fives," Chris said.

"All for one and one for all," Gadget added.

The gang scrambled for the list. Stretch was the first to find his name. "I'm on the list and so are you," he said to Chris.

"All right!" Jack cheered. "I'm up there."

"Hey, J.R.'s still up there, too," Chris said.

J.R. smiled. "Coach said if I wanted to stay on, he'd really like me to help."

Jack teasingly rubbed his knuckles into his brother's head. "You knew all afternoon, you punk."

Only Gadget was still staring blankly at the list. "I don't get it," he said.

"Didn't you make the squad?" Stretch's voice was quiet.

"Oh, yeah, see right there? Gadget Shaw, special teams and back-up quarterback."

"That's great," Jack said, starting to lift him up off the ground.

"Alex is up there, too," Gadget continued.

"So what are you so bummed about?" Chris wondered. "The High-Fives have done it again." They all screamed and cheered except Gadget.

"What about Charlie? His name isn't on the list. You didn't tell the coach about your drug investigation, did you?"

"No, of course not," Jack said, looking at the list.

Stretch checked the squad again. "I don't get it."

"He's the best player on the team." Gadget walked to the coach's office and poked his head in. The others followed. "We're all really happy about making the team, Coach Halligan, but why isn't Charlie Palmer's name on the list?"

"Come on in, boys. Charlie's dad was here earlier, and it seems his business in Texas is thriving again, so the family is going back to Houston before school starts."

"Thanks, Coach, I guess that makes sense." Gadget and the others walked out of the office.

"Let's give him a call and ask him to meet us at Mike's for root beer and fries," Chris suggested.

"Alex, too," J.R. added.

"We've got a lot of celebrating to do," Jack added.

"Yeah." Gadget smiled. "As seventh graders."

About the Author

S. S. GORMAN grew up in Greeley, Colorado, with two older brothers and two younger brothers. The family was always active in sports. Their favorites included skiing, skating, softball, golf, tennis, swimming, hiking, fishing, basketball, and football. Ms. Gorman has a B.S. degree from Colorado State University and an M.A. from the University of Northern Colorado. For the past ten years she has worked as a professional performer on stage and in radio and film, as well as writing several young-adult novels. The titles in *The High-Fives* series are: SOCCER IS A KICK, SLAM DUNK, HOME RUN STRETCH, and QUARTERBACK SNEAK, available from Minstrel Books. She currently lives in New York City with her husband and two children.

JAMIE GILSON KEEPS YOU LAUGHING!